Dedicated to my parents, for their endless support and sacrifices, regardless of circumstance.

With thanks to my brother Matt for helping me invent the characters and find their voices.

THE TENDER WALL

by
Tim Whitehouse

PART ONE

The White Room – Sam

"Please state your name."

Sam jumped in her seat at the disembodied voice. She found herself in a white room, the main feature of which was its total lack of features. No corners, no doors, no windows: just a gently glowing white space, although she could not work out exactly where the light was coming from.

Her seat was similarly featureless – not quite a chair, not quite a bed, it was perfectly moulded to her body. Her legs were raised as though in a dentist's chair, and she was comfortable, but the voice caused her to sit up. As she did, the chair moved with her, providing perfect support without any visible means of adjustment.

"Where am I?" she asked, searching the room in vain for some sort of clue.

"Please state your name," the voice repeated. It was a woman's voice: firm but warm.

"I'm sorry, but you can't just keep me in this weird white room and quiz me like this. I have no idea who you are or where I am. I'd like to know what's going on, please."

"All in good time. Please start by stating your name."

Sam let out a deep sigh and hunched her shoulders,

rubbing her arms and squeezing herself tight, partly for comfort, partly for safety. She looked around the room for clues as she reflected on her situation. There was nothing, with no idea where she was, nor memory of how she'd got there, she decided to comply.

"Fuller. Sam. Samantha. Sorry, I mean it's Samantha Fuller. My name." Sam stumbled over her words.

"Please explain how you came to be here."

"I don't even know where here is!"

"Please explain how you came to be here."

"I'm really not sure. Where am I? I've just woken up in a very strange place, and you're demanding an explanation... maybe if you gave me some more information, I'd be able to answer."

She noticed her outfit, an all-in-one, close-fitting, stretchy white garment, like an adult baby-grow. She gently rubbed her arms and explored the rest of her body as if checking for injuries, the only change being that her thick black curls were tied back.

"Also, where are my clothes?"

"Please explain how you came to be here. Start with the last thing you remember."

Sam took a moment to consider her options, quickly realising that she didn't really have any.

Giving the voice the benefit of the doubt, she closed her eyes. "I remember being with my mum, it was Bonfire Night."

5th November, 2050hrs

Sam stood on the banks of the River Thames, huddled close to her mother, Val. They were both wrapped up in scarves and heavy coats to fight the November cold. As the ever-present stench of stale urine burned their nostrils they pulled their scarves up over their noses, dropping them to speak. Public conveniences had been the first thing to go when the landlords took control of London.

Across the river, the new city wall loomed over them, hiding the office blocks and luxury apartments inside, or more specifically, hiding the decaying city from the ruling class within.

As fireworks burst above the wall, a large crowd on the banks cooed with delight. Sam tightened her grip on Val's arm, keeping her eye on the sky as they spoke.

"He used to hate fireworks, didn't he?" Val said wistfully, a look of sadness in her eyes.

"I know, it's ironic, isn't it?" Sam replied.

"Remember when you were doing that charity thing at school and they wanted to spend all that money on a firework display?"

"Ha! Yeah, he went mad! Said we might as well burn the money."

"Yeah. Hey, do you think we'd have got back

together? You know, if the attack hadn't happened?"

"Who knows? Maybe... What time is it?" Sam loosened her grip slightly; she didn't like talking about her dad's death.

"I do miss him though, it would just be nice to know he was there if we needed him, wouldn't it?"

Sam looked at the ground without answering, grappling with unspoken thoughts. Val pulled back her glove to look at her watch and took a deep breath.

"It's nearly nine."

"I've got to go; I've got work," replied Sam.

"Are you going to the vigil?"

"I don't think so. You?"

"My wall pass expired."

"OK, see you in the morning then. I'll be quiet when I get in."

"See you later, love."

Sam leaned in for a hug, kissed her mum on the cheek, and made her way towards the checkpoint she'd need to pass in order to enter the walls. Motionless armed guards, lined the bridge, their bodies and faces hidden by combat armour. *Props*, as they were generally referred to, was short for *Property Guardians*, a company set up at the turn of the century to prevent squatters from taking over empty buildings. It had once been a good way to find cheap rent in London, but as the housing crisis had taken hold, potential squatters became more forceful. Initially, the Property Guardians were offered self-defence lessons in an attempt to stay safe from would-be attackers. When this became insufficient, they were offered basic weapons training. Eventually, they became a private army, patrolling the streets, executing evictions, and generally protecting the interests of the landlords.

"They could be mannequins and no one would know." thought Sam, not that she'd be willing to test that theory.

The booms and whistles continued as she crossed the bridge, the smoke in the air catching the coloured light of the fireworks. Coupled with the military presence, it was easy to pretend she was in a war zone. Even in the slums, fireworks were going off. Sam couldn't help but wonder how people with so little were so keen to waste their money on lame fireworks.

At the end of the bridge was the first barrier, a turnstile with a touchpad. She rummaged through her many layers of pockets and produced an ID card on the end of a lanyard, which she raised to the touchpad. With a mechanical clunk, the turnstile gave way, allowing her access to the last section.

She joined a short queue of people waiting to enter. This was the service entrance to the city; they didn't just let anybody through. Razor wire lined the bridge barriers and the tops of the security huts. At the sides of the path, poles rose with so many CCTV cameras and speakers attached they started to look like futuristic Christmas trees.

Approaching the gate, she passed through an X-ray machine before being patted down by a faceless guard – pointlessly, given the number of layers she was wearing.

As she walked, a gun turret with a camera attached picked her out and followed her path. This was a *Sentry,* an automated defence system that could be set to identify and hold, or even kill, wanted terrorists using facial recognition. She knew she had nothing to worry about, but nonetheless, having a gun follow you was disconcerting to say the least.

Waiting in line for the final check, she looked up at the dark, towering wall. From her perspective, it appeared to rise endlessly, like an insurmountable black cliff face. At regular intervals, large, slow-moving rotor blades were set into the wall, presumably keeping the pollution at bay.

Occasionally, the silhouettes of Sentries along the walls would be highlighted by the fireworks, a reminder of the attempted "Renter's Revolution", after which the landlords isolated themselves from their tenants for fear of their lives.

At the last checkpoint, a stony-faced attendant stood behind a protective screen.

"Pass." he demanded.

Sam handed over a laminated ID card, her work pass: the key to earning a living within the walls. The attendant examined the pass through narrowed eyes, scrutinising the likeness repeatedly as though looking for a reason to turn her back.

"Where are you working?" he asked.

"Dynasty Tower. Cleaning."

The attendant inserted her card into a slot by the screen set into his desk. He waited a moment... a green light came on accompanied by a harsh buzz. He waved her on without another word. Sam pushed through the next turnstile to enter central London.

Inside the walls, everything felt different. It was immaculately clean and tidy, maintained by an army of automated cleaning robots that glided gracefully to remove even the tiniest specks of debris. Overhead, drones carried gourmet meals for delivery, their soft hum barely heard above the city's soundscape.

The lucky few that lived within the walls gathered in bars and restaurants, unfazed by the troubles that plagued the outside world, as they revelled in the pleasure of al fresco dining, protected from the cold by invisible heat sources.

These were the Landlords, the people that owned the buildings and land. Since the end of the 20th century, the landlord class had been consolidating its grip on the country. The scarcity of property kept the value high, meaning fewer and fewer people had been able to buy houses. Private landlords squeezed their tenants dry, using their profits to amass more property (while their tenants moved ever further from saving for property of their own) until the point where only inheritance conferred homeownership. It was like a game of Monopoly where one or two players had played a few rounds alone, buying up all the property before allowing anyone else to join the game.

An attempted rebellion had taken place ten years previously, with a drone attack putting a huge hole in the Houses of Parliament, but the authoritarian government took this as a sign that they were not authoritarian enough. They introduced draconian measures to protect the Landlords by creating a separate city, London within London, where the landlords and corporations were based, closely monitoring the few tenants they allowed in to provide services. Immediately after the Bonfire Night attack, generators and solar panels were rounded up and confiscated - any further rebellions were quickly quashed by turning off the power and water outside the walls, or shutting down the fuel supply.

The biggest of the corporations was Dynasty, a conglomerate of energy companies, security services, AI systems, home delivery companies, prisons, manufacturing companies, and communications networks. They were known for being shady, but also held the majority of government contracts and never seemed to be properly investigated if things went wrong.

Naturally, the biggest of corporations had the biggest of buildings: Destiny Tower stood tall and imposing, a reflective monolith in celebration of capitalism, its perfectly smooth exterior broken up only by a line of gun turrets along the roof and the exterior lifts, speeding fifty storeys up, and down into pitch-black tunnels sinking deep into the ground. The mirrored exterior kept hidden the murky dealings within, whilst allowing its residents to monitor the world outside.

Sam was well aware that she was working for the devil, but even if the money sucked, it was an easy job and there were precious few of them around. She flashed her pass and a smile at the doorman, then waited patiently as the huge revolving door rotated to allow her into the opulent entrance.

The grand atrium was a breathtaking expanse, boasting a soaring, cathedral-like ceiling adorned with ornate chandeliers that cast a soft golden glow across the entire area. Imposing marble columns, polished to a mirror-like sheen, punctuated the walls, lending an air of classical elegance to the modern surroundings.

A lavish carpet unfurled beneath an array of meticulously sculpted potted plants, creating a vibrant, organic contrast to the polished stone and glass. Never-ending windows stretched upwards, offering glimpses of the surrounding cityscape, a tantalising reminder of the corporate power nesting within. A grand reception desk, resplendent with gleaming brass accents, took centre stage, behind which an impeccably dressed concierge tipped his hat to Sam as she skipped by and smiled.

Her work was on the first floor, a much less impressive part of the building: what they did there was a mystery to her. Rows of indistinguishable cubicles stretched endlessly, each housing a solitary computer and little else. She emptied a few bins, vacuumed the messy bits, and then, having previously managed to acquire a computer password through the power of flirting, got to work on the latest assignment for her Economics degree.

Wincing slightly at the essay title she'd been set, she typed it into the search engine: "Why do fossil fuels provide a more stable economy than traditional renewable energy?"

Her cursor hovered over the first link that came up. A handsome lad in his twenties was giving her a cocky wink from the thumbnail, sitting on a bed with a large "De-bunk Bed" logo behind him. Impressed by the view count, which was well over a million, she clicked and picked up her notepad as the young man made his introduction in an affected estuary accent:

"Welcome to De-Bunk Bed, thanks for subscribing. Unless you haven't, in which case, why not? My name's Jack Klein, and this week I'll be sorting more fact from fallacy as we look into all these tremors we've been having recently…" He grabbed the table and shook it, simulating an earthquake.

"CAN YOU FEEL THAT??" he yelled at the camera. He was cocksure in a way that Sam did not particularly like, although she thought she might be able to get over it for that cheeky smile…

"No? Well, you've got your head in the clouds! Come down here and put your ear to the ground, because there's a-rumblin' beneath these streets and, as we all know, it ain't the Victoria Line! Is it fracking, or… could this be the work of The UnHeard? If the reports showing fracking is safe are true, who do we blame? Or is it just little old Earth telling us she's had enough?"

Pen in hand, Sam watched with half-hearted interest, trying to stay focused enough to make use of anything useful he might have to say. However, despite Jack's exuberance, it had been a long day and, despite her best intentions, she gently drifted off to sleep.

The White Room – Jack

"Please state your name."

Jack opened his eyes and looked from side to side, remaining motionless. He grimaced, rubbed his eyes, and pushed his tousled hair back.

Sitting up, he took in the situation. There were no clues to be found in the room; there was nothing to be found. He pulled at the stretchy white onesie he was wearing.

"Where are my clothes?"

"Please state your name."

"Hey, you can't just go around undressing people, you know. What's going on? Oh hang on, this is a prank, isn't it? You're wasting your time, you know. I'm signed. You have to pay rights if you want to use me for clicks; you'll get sued otherwise."

This was mostly untrue, but Jack sounded completely sure of what he was saying, one of his genuine talents.

"Please state your name."

"Coffee." he demanded.

"Name: Coffee."

"No, I... have you got coffee? Can I have some coffee? Please?"

CLUNK. The lights shut off. PSSST. CLUNK. The lights came back on and a tall, elegant glass with dark liquid had appeared on the arm of his chair.

Pleased, Jack settled back into his chair, slightly disconcerted by the way it adjusted to his movements.

"Thank you. Where were we? You wanted my name, right? It's Jack. Jack Klein."

He leaned forward and took a sip of the drink, then, slightly puzzled, he looked into the glass, then through the glass, then up to the ceiling where he presumed the person he was speaking to would be based.

"This isn't coffee." He took another sip. "It's amazing though, what is it?"

There was no response, so being quite used to talking into the void, he carried on.

"So, what is this, some sort of government facility? I like it, you've got that whole clean lines, feng shui thing going on. Slightly sterile... you could do with some plants, maybe a throw..."

"Please explain how you came to be here."

"You're really nailing this atonal androgynous vibe. Listen, am I in trouble or...? You can't just keep me locked up, I've got over a million followers, they'll want to know where I am."

"Please explain how you came to be here. Start with the last thing you remember."

"Now you mention it, I'm not fully sure how I got here. I feel pretty hungover; there must have been drinking. I remember being in the pub with Owen, so that would make sense…"

5th November, 2345hrs

Jack sat in the Old Queen's Head, one of the few pubs that had managed to keep its doors open outside the walls. A band was playing classical dance tunes from the turn of the century using shoddy acoustic guitars, thumping out the beat on a wooden box.

The locals were celebrating. Bonfire Night always brought out their party spirits, despite having nothing much to cheer: perhaps it was the bright lights from the fireworks, breaking through the smog and making their world a little less grey. Maybe it was the thought of dealing a blow to the Landlords, not that it had helped them much in the long run.

The bar was packed and buzzing, filled with people of all ages drinking from home-brewed barrels of grog which sat on the bar top. Hands slapped tables in time with the music, older people sang along when the chorus kicked in, remembering a better time.

A flickering TV screen showed a crowd of people holding candles in Parliament Square, outside a scaffold-wrapped House of Commons. The reporter spoke solemnly:

"It was a night in British history that will never be forgotten. On the tenth anniversary of the horrific

attack on Parliament, a midnight vigil remembers those who lost their lives at the hands of The UnHeard."

Jack sat with Owen, a stocky but neatly presented Welshman, monologuing loudly, as though for the benefit of the pub, rather than just Owen. Dressed in his trademark hoodie and long messy hair, it was hard to believe it was Jack that employed Owen.

"All I'm saying," Jack slurred, "is that a bit of perspective wouldn't hurt. People get so riled up over such little things these days. Like with bees."

"Bees?" asked Owen, without looking up from his phone.

"Yeah, bees. Everyone goes on about saving them. It's not that big a deal - just eat syrup! Problem solved. It's not like most of us can afford honey anyway." Jack crossed his arms and sat back triumphantly.

"No, Jack…"

"And they sting. Not only that, but stinging is like suicide for them and they still do it. Talk about holding a grudge!"

"Jack, that's not the thing with bees. At all." Owen's patience was legendary.

"What, that they don't sting or that they don't make honey. I think you'll find you're wrong on both counts."

"How do you not know this?" asked Owen, almost annoyed, but genuinely interested. "Bees pollinate the plants. If plants don't pollinate, we don't get food."

"What, really?" Jack was taken aback by this news. "That would make all the complaining more reasonable, I suppose. What about wasps, the little stingy twats?"

"They fertilise figs." Owen continued doomscrolling.

"Bullshit."

"Look it up, mate. Every fig has a wasp inside."

"Gross! That's the last time I ever eat a fig!"

"Ha!" This tickled Owen. "When have you ever eaten a real fig? That's strictly Landlord food."

"I might one day if I sell another story." Jack fell silent for a moment as he allowed this newfound knowledge to sink in. "Do all insects and animals have a job then?"

"Yeah, it's the ecosystem, innit? This eats that, which fertilises that and so on."

"Right, course, yeah." Jack paused again and furrowed his brow. "What do humans do?"

"Ah well, now you're asking." Owen looked up for the first time. "Nothing good."

"What, nothing?"

"Nada. Maybe our ancient ancestors did, but not now. We just consume."

"What, so we're worse than wasps?"

"Good band name. Worse Than Wasps."

"Well, I guess we're going to go extinct one way or another. If it's all for honey, then that's as good a way as any." Jack sat back, content with this conclusion.

Owen shook his head slightly and returned to his phone, as Jack swiftly forgot what they were talking about and started a whole new conversation.

"Hey, are you on 'Harker'? See if there's been any attacks."

"There's no need to sound so hopeful!" said Owen, raising his eyebrows and looking at Jack for the first time in a while.

"Oh come on... you know we need the business." teased Jack.

"I'm sorry, I didn't realise we were undertakers now."

"It may have escaped your notice, mate, but terrorism sells. And our numbers are down..."

"It's propaganda and you know it."

"Yeah, well, it's paying for this proper lager, so stop your moaning."

"Speaking of which..." Owen waved his glass in the air and mimed choking.

"Bollocks, I bought the last three!"

"You're the only one with money."

"You get paid!" Jack said with mock incredulity.

"Yeah, by you."

Jack stood up and patted down his thighs, signifying that he'd run out of cash.

"And the cupboard was bare... have you got nothing at all?"

Owen begrudgingly patted himself down, making a show of pulling out the pockets of his neatly kept chinos and Harrington jacket, throwing tatty bits of paper and plastic discs onto the table as he found them. Jack examined the results and looked up in disbelief.

"That's it? Four food stamps and a work coupon? Do they even take food stamps here?"

"Sorry, mate, we can't all be gifted the scoop of the century. You need to spread the love."

"Parasite."

An attractive girl approached their table, instantly distracting Jack from their lack of funds.

"Excuse me," she smiled coyly as she spoke.

"Yes, yes. It is me," Jack sighed, this was all part of being a grassroots celebrity. "Selfie, is it?"

"Sorry?" The girl was nonplussed.

"Autograph then? Old school, I like it."

Jack reached into Owen's bag and pulled out a headshot with a large logo reading 'De-Bunk Bed' across the top. The girl looked over her shoulder at her friend, confused as Jack started writing. Jack put his winning smile into action as he handed her the photograph.

"I stuck my number on there too. You know, should you need it…"

He winked as he handed her the photo. The girl glanced at Owen, then back to her friend, taking the photo only to put it back on the table.

"No, the chair. Can I take the chair?"

She pointed to an empty chair tucked under their table. Jack looked down and coughed, stuffing the picture into his hoodie pocket as Owen tried to suppress his laughter.

Without looking back up, he replied, "Yeah, take it. We're leaving anyway."

Jack clumsily pushed himself to his feet, his unsteady legs letting him down as he staggered backwards. He toppled over his own chair, landing with a crash on the adjacent table. The unfortunate punters watched in dismay as their drinks cascaded in all directions.

As an angry owner of the spilled drinks got to his

feet, Owen reacted with lightning speed, seizing Jack by the arm and steering him out of the bar, away from trouble. The locals might be the so-called 'salt of the Earth', but outside of the fortified walls, the world was a tough and unforgiving place, where survival often trumped camaraderie and there was little room for forgiving waste.

Outside the tattered bar, the towering walls cast an ominous shadow over Islington. Between the fans, massive LED screens bathed the urban landscape in an eerie, perpetual glow, broadcasting an endless barrage of news, empty politician's speeches, and adverts. This was the main vessel for disseminating information, or propaganda as some might see it: new laws, new restrictions, rarely anything positive. They were best suited to peddling falsehoods, designed to maintain an iron grip on the collective psyche.

The streets themselves were a twisted labyrinth of makeshift shelters, composed of discarded pallets and scavenged street furniture, all interconnected by a web of dangerously fizzing power cables. A ramshackle line of tents marked the divide between cracked pavements and pothole-ridden roads, the standard lot for a community which had abandoned the hope of secure housing.

Most of the shops were boarded up by now, useful only to squatters, with the few operational businesses covered in metal grills and barbed wire, advertising work tokens and food stamps for sale or loan. The street was quiet apart from a few old drunks sitting around a small fire in a defunct shopping trolley.

Owen still had hold of Jack's shoulder. "Are you pissed? You're waking me up tomorrow, right?"

"Yes, I am," Jack grinned.

"Pissed or waking me up?"

"Exactly."

Across the road, four teenage lads bowled around the corner, boisterously pushing one another around, jumping on each other's backs, and generally being far too rowdy for the time of night.

As Jack and Owen came into their eyeline, the tallest of the group stopped in his tracks, pulling his mate back and whispering in his ear. They started muttering to one another, swinging furtive glances towards Jack and Owen and becoming more and more animated.

The tall lad shouted: "Oi Jack! Jack Off! Off to De-Wank-Bed?"

He made lewd gestures around his crotch as the other lads cheered and laughed. To Owen's disappointment, Jack returned the gesture. Realising this needed nipping in the bud, Owen stepped forward.

"Alright kids. Fuck off home to mummy, yeah?"

The lads crossed the road towards them, reaching into their coats to pull out various homemade weapons: sticks, rocks, a catapult. Owen stood in front of Jack, limbering up with arm stretches before taking a boxing stance.

"You really think you're up to this boys?"

The boys laughed and pulled out a selection of small fireworks, huddling around the one lad with a lighter to spark the fuses.

WHIZZ! BANG! A bright ball of flames shot between Owen and Jack, sending them to the ground. Jack started to panic, thinking back to the videos he'd seen in school.

"Owen, do something! I can't do my show if I'm all burned up and disfigured. My face is our fortune."

"Yeah, right," mumbled Owen under his breath.

A second firework screamed past, bouncing haphazardly off the walls and setting light to a tent. Sheltering Jack with one arm, Owen pulled him behind an abandoned car as a barrage of missiles rained down on them.

"YOU LOT ARE DEAD!" yelled Owen, looking for an opportunity to attack.

One of the younger lads who had disappeared now returned with a length of corroded drainpipe, which he dutifully placed on his shoulder as the tallest boy placed a massive firework inside. Eager and wild-eyed, the younger boy aimed his improvised rocket launcher at Jack as the older boy lit the fuse.

A flicker of panic surged through Jack and Owen as they realised their vulnerable position. These boys were probably just playing, but fireworks could seriously injure and nobody likes burns.

Desperately, they tried to make it back to the pub before the fuse was spent. As they ran for the door, the rocket screamed between them with a piercing squeal, narrowly missing Jack's head and shooting through the pub window.

BOOM! A thunderous explosion came from inside the pub, far beyond anything you'd expect from a firework. CRASH! The ground rumbled and shook beneath, throwing Jack sprawling to the ground just a few feet from the door.

A deafening cacophony of metal distorting and scraping filled the air, like a million nails scratching a chalkboard at once, before the pub imploded, disappearing into the ground in a ball of dust and smoke and taking the punters with it.

Left behind was nothing but rubble, broken glass, bricks, and scorched earth, surrounding a seemingly bottomless sinkhole, an abyss which had seemingly eaten a building whole.

The boy with the drainpipe was stunned, unable to make sense of the carnage, while his friends ran for their lives. He was rooted to the spot.

Around the edge of the gaping hole, a few jagged remnants of the pub floor had escaped the wreck, but with a wall on one side and a hole on the other, the survivors in those areas were left holding on desperately as more of the floor gave way. Others found themselves trapped by fallen beams or missing limbs, severed as the floors above them crumbled.

Jack raised his head from the rubble and took in the chaos of this post-apocalyptic scene. Standing up, he dusted himself down, instantly sober, and urgently grabbed Owen's arm to help him up.

"Terrorists!"

Without hesitating, Owen grabbed his backpack, took out a remote control drone, and attached a small camera. With the flick of a switch, the drone whirred into life and Owen took control.

Content that Owen was getting all the footage they'd need, Jack called his Editor-in-Chief.

Bill, a balding, single man in his late fifties, was snoring, sheets heaped on one side of the bed, pizza boxes littering the room. He had no trousers on but still wore a stained shirt and tie as he slept, cradling an empty whisky bottle. On his wall were framed photographs of his younger self with politicians and royalty, a reminder of his glory days as a BBC broadcaster.

Bill stirred slowly, barely responding to his phone's ring. He moved his feet to the floor, sitting on the edge of his bed and rubbing his head before reaching to answer. Seeing that the incoming call was from Jack, his thumb hovered over the reject button for a moment before reluctantly accepting the call.

"This had better be good, Jack."

"Bill! I got one mate. You won't believe what just happened…"

"Alien invasion? The Rapture? Armageddon?"

"Nope - even better!"

"Jack, are you in a bar? You sound like you're in a bar."

"Technically I am not in a bar. Anyway, that's not the point… there's been another attack - like, a big one! There are dead people, wrecked buildings, the works!"

"You sound genuinely pleased."

"I'm right in the middle of it! There's - wait I'll show you, I'm switching to video."

Jack hung up and fiddled with his phone as an armed surveillance drone hovered into view over the bewildered crowd, broadcasting a tannoy message:

"*Citizens! For your own safety and the safety of others, martial law has now been imposed in section 271. Please leave the area immediately and return to your homes.*"

"What homes?" called a voice from the gathering crowd.

The chaos was soon punctuated by the military precision of a fleet of armoured black vehicles, delivering a swarm of guards, filing out of the sliding doors like cockroaches from a disrupted nest. The Props raised their riot shields and fired warning shots skywards, the sharp report of their weapons cracking the air as they forced back concerned onlookers.

Now on a video call, Jack held his phone up high, allowing Bill to take in the full extent of the wreckage. He stumbled through the chaos, capturing the walking wounded and relentless Props. Struggling to steady his hand, he zoomed in on an unfortunate victim, bleeding and trapped under a mess of rubble and twisted rebar.

Bill covered his mouth, upset by what he saw but with no words, as Jack's face appeared on-screen, a backdrop of devastation framing his inappropriately eager expression.

"Are you seeing this?"

"Yes, I'm seeing it. Very graphic…"

"I know, right?"

"Have you got Owen with you?"

Jack looked smug.: "Yeah, he's getting footage now…"

Jack turned the phone to show Owen arguing with a Prop.

"Hang on, coppers are here…" Jack took a moment to hear what was happening.

"OI! GET THAT DRONE OUT OF HERE!" ordered an officer.

Owen cockily flashed a permit at the policeman.

"Er… licence!"

"I don't care if you're the royal photographer, mate. Stop shooting before I start!" the officer put a hand on his gun as he said this.

Jack felt the need to interject:

"FASCIST!" he yelled, before turning back to Bill: "What do you reckon? This is a national job, right? It's got to be The UnHeard…"

"We don't know that, Jack."

"Oh come on, who else would do this?"

Bill held his phone to his chest for a moment, considering the situation. Jack had a tendency to jump to conclusions, but he was the first reporter on-site and that sort of lead should never be ignored.

"I'll tell you what - if you can have a piece ready by 5am, I'll make sure it gets to Head Office. It's their call."

"Done. This is going to be huge!"

Jack jogged enthusiastically over to Owen, who was now filming without his drone.

"Bill says we can go for national news if we have it ready by 5am. I'll get a couple of interviews, then I'm off to the office."

"Sweet, got your eye on anyone? What about that kid with the drainpipe?" Owen pointed to the only remaining gang member.

A tremor caused the ground to shake again – Owen and Jack looked at each other nervously.

"Bombs don't have aftershocks, mate," Owen pointed out.

"Yeah, well... the boss has spoken and we need to get paid."

Jack pulled out his phone, opened "Harker," and composed a message:

"CAUGHT UP IN AN EXPLOSION! CHECK HERE FOR FULL REPORT #PULLINGANALLNIGHTER #CHAINEDTOMYDESK"

He clicked on the "HARK" icon to post his status update.

6th November, 0030hrs

Sam was still in the office when the shouting woke her from her sleep. It took a moment for her to adjust and realise that she wasn't at home. As she came to her senses, she noticed it was darker than she'd expected. She checked the time on her phone – after midnight! She should not still be there; it was well past curfew, so she shouldn't even have been within the walls! Judging by the tone of the voices, she most definitely did not want to explain herself to the approaching men.

Her instinct was to drop to the floor and hide under the desk, hoping they might pass through. Then she could sneak out, leaving just the security guard to deal with. A smile and a wave would be fine for him; they'd always been friendly. As the voices grew louder, she peeped through a gap in the desk to figure out when it would be safe to move.

A tall, intimidating man in his late forties, with chiselled, angry features, a bald head, and a sharp suit, walked quickly through the office. He was followed by a distressed office worker who was trying to keep up and explain himself, apparently unsuccessfully.

The bald man was clearly the boss, an unpleasant one at that:

"I don't care whose fault it is, I need power to the

Bunker, now!"

"Please, Mr Lawson sir, forget the power failure – this is much worse!" the office worker pleaded.

Lawson stopped and exhaled heavily, pinching the bridge of his nose as he did so.

"Sorry sir, but the thing is, well, it's Pandora…"

Lawson looked back at the man sharply, a touch of alarm in his eyes.

"Pandora?"

"It's out sir, or at least it's about to be. We need to warn people!"

"No, that's impossible. We took every precaution, how could that happen?"

"It's because of FLEM, sir. The surveyors must have missed something… a new fault line opened up unexpectedly, way off course, and hit the facility."

"How certain are you of this?"

"100% sir, when the next quake hits it will open up the fault completely… the containment facility won't stand up to it, Pandora will be released."

"Next quake?"

The man pulled out a USB stick and thrust it into Lawson's chest, quickly retracting it when Lawson's glare told him he'd overstepped.

"Yes sir, about noon tomorrow, we think. It's all

on here. We have no protocol for this, sir."

"There's always a protocol. What about the staff?"

"All dead – the emergency system sealed them inside. I'm going to contact the press, we have to warn the public!"

"Who else knows about this?"

"No one yet, I came straight to you."

"Good."

Lawson hit the man hard in the throat with the edge of his open hand, breaking his windpipe, then quietly, expertly smothered the man's mouth as he dropped to his knees, pulling his head into his hips as he tried to draw breath.

Sam struggled to suppress a gasp of horror as she realised she was witnessing a murder, momentarily forgetting the impending disaster the man had died over.

With his hand still over his victim's mouth, Lawson lifted his wrist and spoke calmly into his watch as his convulsing victim eventually went limp and crumpled to the floor.

"Clean up, first floor reception."

Lawson took the USB stick and stood up, straightening his suit jacket as he did so, then headed in Sam's direction. As he made his way towards her, Sam crawled under desks and between chairs, trying her best not to make a sound as she went. This was going to be tricky; the exit was at the end of a straight corridor with two doors and an elevator she'd need to pass.

Through a gap in the office dividers, Sam could see Lawson's feet. She paused, waiting to see where he would go next. To her horror, he went nowhere, instead plugging the USB stick into the nearest computer and starting to open files, his back to the corridor.

Poking her head out from under the desk, Sam saw her chance to escape. She slowly edged towards the exit, her back flat against the wall, with Lawson busily going through documents with his back to her.

PING! The sound of the elevator arriving took her by surprise, but Lawson didn't flinch. Looking from side to side for a place to hide, the only option she found was a door marked "CONFERENCE 1". She pushed through quickly but quietly and edged the blind away from a small window, allowing her to see into the corridor.

Two cleaners in full HAZMAT suits came out of the lift, pushing a large trolley and a stretcher along the corridor.

"Clean up, sir."

"Very good. Move quickly." He gestured towards the lifeless body, slumped behind the reception desk.

Sam took in her surroundings; she didn't clean this room. The conference room was small with a highly polished semi-circular table, its flat edge pushed up to the wall opposite the door, five tall mahogany chairs around it. Holding her breath, she stayed motionless, listening for evidence that the coast was clear and she could escape. Putting her ear to the door, she heard footsteps approaching. Her eyes got wider as the steps got louder, eventually stopping right outside.

Realising they were probably coming in, she desperately looked for a place to hide. The door opened just as she disappeared under the table and pulled the chair behind her, and Lawson entered.

"Connect to The Lodge," he said.

"Connecting," replied a synthetic voice.

The walls of the room flickered into life, transforming the formerly featureless walls into a three-dimensional canvas as the plush yet businesslike image of a boardroom materialised. The walls adopted a velvety texture, exuding an aura of both luxury and professionalism.

The semi-circular table now stretched out to form an oval, its glass-like surface reflecting the soft, ambient light. Five chairs became ten, their quilted red leather cushioning inviting participants to sit for hours in comfort.

A sinewy man in his late sixties, wearing silk pyjamas and a robe, was standing with his back to the table, facing news footage of a small riot on a TV screen. He watched without interest, switching channels with a swiping gesture. The screen showed more scenes of civic unrest.

As Lawson's 3D avatar appeared in the room, the man switched the screen off with a downward gesture and turned away to look out of the window.

"I hope this is important."

"I'm afraid it is, sir. There's been an accident; Pandora is out of the box. We've contained it for now, but we need to make preparations."

The man turned to look at Lawson. "I see. What's the recommendation?"

"Alternative three, sir."

The man turned to face Lawson for the first time, one eyebrow raised. "Alternative three? And you're quite sure about that, are you?"

"Absolutely. We can't afford to wait."

"Timescale?"

"The situation's already critical, sir. We have just under twelve hours before our safety measures become worthless."

Lawson leaned over slightly, inserting the USB drive into a slot in the desk and typing into a screen now projected on the desk. "The files are on your system now, sir. With your permission, I'll start making arrangements."

"Well, I suppose we always knew this day would come. Initiate The Phoenix Protocol. Contact those that matter."

"Yes, sir."

"We're going to need the proles out of the way."

"Leave it with me, sir."

"Today will be an interesting day… One other thi-"

A small tremor shook the building. With a flash, the power went out, and the room instantly returned to the blank canvas it had been.

"DAMMIT!"

Lawson rushed out of the now pitch-black room, leaving Sam alone. Using her phone for light, she climbed out from under the desk, her eyes landing on the USB stick still in the slot. Without thinking, she pulled it out and thrust it deep inside her pocket. This was her chance: while the lights were still out, she gently opened the door and felt her way along the corridor until she made it to the fire exit. Holding her breath, she pushed the bar slowly, waiting to hear the click of the lock before slipping through the smallest of gaps. Just as the door shut behind her, the lights came back on, but she was on her way.

The external fire exit door was alarmed, but she

didn't have time to worry about that. She clattered through the door and ran, pulling her coat over her head to avoid the cameras and disappeared into the night.

6th November, 0500hrs

Jack sat at a desk in the newsroom, busily stitching together footage from the pub. This was no Sky News; the office was a mess: empty pizza boxes, dirty coffee cups and half-eaten Pot Noodles accounted for the majority of the desk space. In pride of place stood a framed photo of Jack with his arm around a sweet-looking old lady.

Jack had hurriedly pushed the detritus into a heap on one side and surrounded himself with camera equipment and photographs of recent bombings. On screen, he had multiple tabs open: articles detailing earthquakes, fracking investigations, and renewable energy were all open. He'd studied all this for his podcast (his award-winning podcast, as Jack insisted it was referred to), in which he'd debunked the many, many conspiracy theories that plagued the country.

He chewed on a pencil, scrolling back and forth through footage of the explosion and his report. Standing in front of the gaping hole where the pub once stood, he spoke into the camera:

"I'm outside a pub in North London, where an explosion has killed at least ten people and seriously injured others. While we don't yet know who's responsible, it bears all the hallmarks of terrorist faction, 'The Unheard.'"

He skipped through footage, stopping on an interview with one of the thugs that had harassed him earlier:

"The floor started shaking really hard, then the whole thing just went."

Jack stopped the video and paused to think. Clicking through the open windows on his screen, he stopped on an old video of a sinkhole swallowing a building in Wales, which was eerily similar to what had happened the previous night.

He clicked between the two images. Could this be something? Over the years, he'd learned that the obvious answer was nearly always the right one. This was obviously terrorism; the timing alone confirmed that. But why target places outside the walls? It was true that the Sentries made missile attacks all but impossible, but innocent people? Who knew what motivated terrorists? It wouldn't be the first time locals had been killed to make a political point.

He mulled it over for a second, then closed the screen, opened his email, attached his report, and pressed send. Done, he could relax. There was a threadbare sofa in the office; he pulled his hood up, drew the strings tight, and put his head down to sleep.

6th November, 0745hrs

Jack was sound asleep when a TAP... TAP... TAP... at the window disturbed him. He sat up and stretched, bleary-eyed, then put his feet on the floor, knocking over a mouldy mug and some food boxes as he did so. He jumped at the clatter and turned to deal with it before noticing the tapping that had woken him.

"What the fuuuuu..."

He stumbled over to the window where a small, tatty old drone with an old mobile phone and a USB drive gaffer-taped to it appeared to be trying to break through. Moving from side to side, he grimaced as he realised the camera was on and following his movements. The phone rang.

"Bit invasive..."

Jack was curious, though, and opened the window to let the drone in. It hovered in front of him, phone ringing, until he plucked it out of the air. He grabbed the phone and flipped it open impatiently, putting it to his ear and tilting the drone to look into the camera.

A woman spoke: "Jack? Jack Klein?"

"Speaking... but you're looking at me, aren't you? So you know that already. Who is this?"

"My name's Sam - I have a story, something

you'll want. Something big."

"Oooh, big? Sorry, babe, I've heard that one before. Sam who, anyway? How did you know I'd be here?"

"It's not hard to find someone who 'HARKS' as much as you do. Listen, the drone - it has a USB drive inside. Can you see the compartment?"

"God, not one for small talk, eh?" He didn't need to see Sam to sense her impatience.

"Can you see it?" she repeated.

Jack turned the drone in his hands, finding a small door in the underside. He pushed it gently and the door flipped open to reveal a USB stick, which he removed, inspecting it from all sides as though it might provide a clue as to what was going on.

"Ok, got it – is this a fan thing? Am I going to find saucy pics on here? Cos you sound quite hot. I can tell by your voice, it's one of my many talents."

He headed to his computer, resting the drone on a desk.

"It's a story," continued Sam, "It's to do with the explosions last night. It's really not safe to talk – please, just do as I say, everything will make sense."

"You're a bit late, to be honest," said Jack as he sat at his computer, drive in hand, "I sent my piece like, three hours ago."

"Trust me, you'll want to know about this."

"OK, bear with me."

He absent-mindedly put the phone down on the desk and pushed the drive into his computer, ignoring Sam as she continued:

"OK, good - now, it's very imp…" Jack clicked to open the file; immediately his computer shut down, "…important that you don't try to open the files on the drive while WIFI is connected."

A message appeared on Jack's screen:

"FATAL ERROR 00001. HACKERS MAY BE TRYING TO ACCESS YOUR DEVICE. YOUR DEVICE HAS BEEN LOCKED FOR YOUR OWN SAFETY. SERVICE WILL BE RESTORED IN 3MIN 27SECS. THANK YOU FOR YOUR PATIENCE."

The time in the message counted down. Jack grabbed the phone, slightly alarmed.

"What just happened?"

"What did you do?" Sam asked.

"It just shut down! What is this? Who are you? Are you trying to hack me…"

"I told you not to open the files! You need to get out of there now! You're being traced! They'll be coming!"

"Who'll be coming? What are you on about? I'm

calling the police."

"Don't do that! Just get out, now! Keep the phone, I'll send instructions."

The line went dead. Jack put the phone down and walked over to the window. He wasn't about to run away on the say-so of some mad stalker. Seeing nothing, he shrugged, returned to his desk and searched for the number of the local police on his phone. He'd soon put a stop to this.

As he waited to be connected to the police, he shuddered at the tinny, scratchy music playing through his phone. Surely it could only have been chosen to reduce the number of reports people made. As his PC rebooted, he tapped his keyboard impatiently, waiting for technology to catch up.

"C'mon, c'mon…"

Outside, a large car could be heard pulling up. Still slightly unnerved by the call from Sam, he slid his chair over to the window and peeked out cautiously. To his surprise, he saw a number of heavily armed Props gathering around the entrance of the studio. He gasped and ducked below the window, pushing his back against the wall.

"No fucking way…"

BANG! BANG! BANG! at the door.

"Shit!"

One thing he knew was that when Props in black

vehicles started beating down doors, things rarely ended well for the person inside. Ducking to stay below the windows, he scurried over to grab the USB stick, then headed for the fire escape. From the top of the stairs, Jack could see shadowy figures through the frosted glass of the fire escape at the rear of the building.

SMASH! An axe came through the fire escape, sending glass flying. Jack doubled back, not sure where to head. Both exits were blocked by very aggressive-looking Props; this must be "Them". He ran back to the window and pulled back the blinds. Pushing his face to the glass, he could see the helmets of three Props waiting to enter through the front door.

THUD! The front door was down, and Props were entering the building from both sides and stampeding up the stairs. Panicking, he opened the window and climbed out, lowering himself onto the roof of the old phone boxes below and staying below the CCTV cameras. He gently closed the window after himself and ducked out of sight just as the first Prop entered the newsroom.

As the last Prop entered the building, he jumped to the ground, crunching broken glass as he landed. For a moment, he thought he'd left his keys inside. Should he run? Checking deeper into his pockets, his fingers touched cold metal, and he pulled the keys from their hiding place.

His fingers might have been hot dogs for all the dexterity they provided as he frantically fumbled with his bicycle chain. He almost yelped with relief when the lock came free, but he held it in, threw the chain over his shoulder, pulled up his hood, and jumped on his bike to make his escape.

Back in the newsroom, the drone camera was still on, quietly filming as five men searched the office. One of them sifted through files on his computer, others were turning desk drawers upside down, another gathered Jack's research. As they realised no one was there, a Prop picked up the drone and looked straight down the camera.

Jack cycled fast, looking over his shoulder anxiously. London was in full daylight by now, but still grey from the smog. The once vibrant streets were a shadow of their former selves, the decayed shop fronts a grim reminder of a brighter past, their windows covered with boards, graffiti, and layers of grime. Fading advertisements from a bygone era clung desperately to broken billboards, their messages now irrelevant.

The existing urban decay was increased by the events of the previous night: some of the buildings had been damaged by the tremors and occasionally Jack had to swerve to avoid huge new potholes in the road and the occasional fallen gargoyle.

As housing had become a problem, people had started building upwards. More ramshackle huts sat on top of five-storey houses, accessed by rickety stairs and ladders, unsafe at the best of times. These had not stood up to the tremors very well; many people were trapped on roofs and called to their neighbours for help.

Rubble and debris littered the pavements, remnants of a city in steep decline. The air was thick with the stench of burning plastic, and the cries of children and families wailed around crushed tents. A group of men stood around the carcass of a rusty car sticking out of a large hole in the ground, arguing over the best way to get it out.

6th November, 0745hrs

The phone he'd been given rang again. Trying to cycle with one hand while answering the call, he swerved to avoid a deep crack in the road, almost losing his balance.

"What have you got me into? Why did Props come?"

"Where are you now?" asked Sam, ignoring Jack's question.

"Just coming up to Dalston Junction."

"Good, you're close. Get to Old Shoreditch Station, I'll meet you inside and explain."

"I can't, I don't have a wall pass."

"That's Shoreditch High Street. You want OLD Shoreditch Station. It's off Brick Lane. Do you know it?"

"Yep, alright," said Jack reluctantly, "See you there in five."

As he cycled, the morning news was showing on the city walls, amplified through tannoys attached to CCTV cameras. Jack stopped for a moment to watch their slick reporter doing things properly.

"Last night a series of explosions shook London and the South-East of England. Local reporter Jack Klein was first at the scene."

"Yes!" yelped Jack, momentarily ecstatic to see his report on the national news. The screen cut to Jack's footage, showing a brief part of the interview but focusing on the injured and dead. Jack punched the air and grinned broadly as he picked up his own phone to call Owen, a reaction that would seem extremely inappropriate to anyone watching him. The phone rang for a while, longer than usual, before an answer came.

"Hello?"

"Owen, you're up, good…"

"Hello? I'm sorry, I can't hear you."

"Owen, it's Jack…" he raised his voice before remembering, "AAARGH! Every fucking time!"

"Only kidding, I'm not here really. Leave a message, I'll get back."

"Mate, you've got to change that message! Call me, shit's going off! We made the wall! We made the wall AND shit's going off! Call me!"

He hung up and looked back up at the big wall screen, composing another message on Harker.

"*WE MADE NATIONAL NEWS! I'M ON THE WALL! #WINNINGATJOURNALISM*"

The news report continued:

"*It appears that terrorist group, The UnHeard, are responsible for the attacks and have issued this video, warning of further violence.*"

The screen cut to a man in a black suit and sad clown mask, sitting in front of a large 'UNHEARD' logo scrawled in paint.

"Your government continues to lie to you. The people of this country are forced to live deeper and deeper in poverty while the landlords get richer. They tell you that the war on terrorism can only be won by suppressing freedom of speech and enforcing segregation.

"We say there is a better way. Once before, we took control of the government's own war machines and turned them on a corrupt parliament. Last night we took control of six Predator drones and turned them on selected targets across the country.

"Innocent lives were lost and for this, we apologise. It is an imperfect war but a necessary one if we are to break free from oppression. With this in mind, we give fair warning that today, we will once again turn this government's own weapons against them and bring down the walls of London."

The video came to an end and cut back to the news studio:

"Police are confident that the threat will be neutralised before any further attacks but are closing the walls today for the protection of the people. Now, for a word from our sponsors, here's..."

As he watched the wall, he became aware of the burning stench of stale urine. He looked around and found a skinny old woman shuffling towards him. She was dressed in a stained, ragged nightdress with a threadbare cardigan over the top. It was November, but she was wearing only one shoe, her bare foot dried, cracked, and gnarly, with blood and scabs covering her heel. As she approached, she raised her hand towards her mouth.

"Goahpap?" she spoke unintelligibly.

"What?" asked Jack, not even trying to hide his disdain. He had no time for crackheads. He knew life was hard, but as far as he could see, crack only made it harder; this woman looked 70 but was probably in her 30s.

"Paaaap. Ya goahpaaaap?" she spoke more slowly but made no more sense.

Jack worked out she was asking for a pipe, as though people in the street just carried crack pipes around with them. He turned his back on her and tried calling Owen again, but got the same stupid voicemail message. The crackhead woman was still holding her hands out and croaking "Paahp" at him, as if asking more times would change the contents of his pockets. He gave up on Owen for now and got back to cycling.

Old Shoreditch Station was a very small, windowless building located just outside the walls, obscured by boards and large coils of razor wire. Graffiti covered every surface, providing a kind of camouflage, a chaotic tapestry of dissent and frustration. A huge UnHeard logo was scrawled across its entire face, a futile cry of protest against the collapse of this once proud community.

He locked his bike to a rusting drainpipe and searched for a way into the building. There had clearly been many attempts to enter and secure the building in the past; it was a patchwork of wooden sheets, corrugated iron, and metal grills. Tugging at the various broken and twisted panels, he found a loose sheet plywood. It was overlapped by a sheet of corrugated iron which he bent back, allowing him to pull the plywood out and create a way inside. As he pulled the board back he recoiled in disgust as he was was hit by a particularly pungent stench of piss, soaked into the plywood over years and released when the board moved. It stood to reason – in a city with this many tents, there was precious little plumbing. Public toilets had been closed years ago under the premise that they were used for drugs, the real reason was a lack of interest in providing public services. The result was that alleys and side streets became open toilets, streets for piss, parks for shit.

Jack composed himself and held his breath as he pushed through the hole he'd created. Inside was dark and damp, the once-bustling hub of commuter activity forgotten by the outside world, the stink of piss replaced by fusty damp. A dim, filtered light barely penetrated the station's interior, the decay and neglect evidenced by cracked tiles and peeling paint. The faintest flicker of lighting provided by sparks from fizzing electrical cables allowed Jack to make out the top of the escalators, tripping over a pile of rubbish as he made his way forward.

The escalator was rusted and broken, the rubber handrail no longer in place. A lopsided strip light occasionally blinked on - at the bottom of the escalator lay a pile of glowing embers. Jack was not the first person here today.

Jack picked his way down the motionless steps, navigating his way over upturned crates and shopping trolleys. With each step, the temperature seemed to drop and a palpable sense of foreboding grew stronger.

The tunnels were dark, but randomly placed piles of burning embers guided his way, highlighting missing wall tiles and dripping, mouldy pipes.

"SAM! SAAAAAAM!"

Jack's voice echoed through the tunnels, repeating ever more quietly until he was left with silence. Touching the wall for guidance, he carried on, regularly looking back over his shoulder in a futile attempt to keep track of his progress.

A distant CRASH, followed by laughter, caused Jack's head to jerk in its direction, heightening his concern. Maybe it was Sam… He continued reluctantly, passing more glowing embers along the way. Feeling his way around a corner, he spotted a burning torch on the wall ahead. He approached, fingers outstretched, ready to take it from its perch.

"PSST!"

Jack froze as he realised the voice came from right behind him. He retracted his hand slowly, shaking slightly.

He could now hear mutters and whispers from other voices, getting louder and multiplying. He turned around slowly, hands up by his shoulders, to see a wiry teenage boy. The youth was filthy and extremely pale, his cheekbones jutting out below his dark, sunken eyes: a Tunnel Troll. Jack knew that when the underground had been shut down, many people, unable to find homes, had taken to the tunnels for shelter. He'd heard rumours of Tunnel Trolls before, but never really had reason to think about them, much less come face to face with one. There was a first time for everything.

The teen Troll stood close to his face. He was skinny but looked tough, and he had two much larger Trolls standing behind him.

"You lost, bruv?" he asked menacingly as he pulled out a long knife. "There's a tax down here. You got something for me?"

Jack was scared and desperately looked for a way

out; this was much more Owen's sort of thing. He shrugged sheepishly, then with a look of recognition, pointed at the biggest, ugliest troll.

"Hey, didn't I date your sister?"

As the first troll looked back at his confused companion, Jack quickly turned and ran into the dark tunnels, clattering from wall to wall, blindly turning corner after corner in a bid to escape. The Trolls were in pursuit, their eyes much more used to the dark.

Jack continued running, blind and out of breath, until THUD! The floor ran out and he fell off a platform and onto the tracks.

"OOF!" The fall seemed to paralyse him for a short time. Had he been alone, he'd have laid still until completely recovered, but the sound of oncoming footsteps forced him to get over it.

Lifting his face off the track, he looked to his left to see an abandoned train. Dragging himself to his feet, he staggered towards the carriage in search of a way in. Despite his panic, he had the presence of mind to run for the far end of the carriage before attempting entry, briefly stopping to try forcing the sliding door along the way. Finding no purchase, he hurried towards the end of the train, stopping at the point where two carriages joined and sliding between them before battling with the rusty, seized-up mechanism.

"JA-ACK! Yeah, bruv, we know who you are…"

called a Troll.

With his arms stretched high above his head, he struggled to force the handle, ineffectively hanging from it with his feet flailing around below. Realising his weight would not be enough, he lifted his feet to the base of the carriage, providing leverage. As he struggled, the salty smell of rusted iron mixed with the musty damp in the tunnel leaving a bitter taste at the back of his mouth. He grimaced as he strained against the latch, and with a final tug, the lock moved and he lost his purchase to fall flat on the tracks, again.

The voices had stopped shouting, now they whispered menacingly as the Trolls crept around the carriage from either side.

"Hey Jack, come back. We only want an autograph."

Jack hoisted himself up once more and gave the door a shove. With the screech of metal scraping against metal, the door yielded, releasing a rush of stale air.

"Jack and Jill went up the hill…"

Jack bent himself over the threshold, belly on the floor, and slid himself into the carriage. A dim, cold light filtered through the cracked windows casting suspicious shadows across the decaying interior. Jack was momentarily transported to travelling on the underground as a child, reminded of a happier time when London was accessible to all.

"To fetch a pail of water…"

The sound of a metal pipe being dragged along the side of the train soon brought him to his senses. In lieu of a better plan, he searched for somewhere to hide.

"Jack fell down and broke his crown…"

He stumbled through the carriages, exhausted and battered from the fall. The Troll's calls echoed through the tunnels behind him.

"And then we kicked his head in!"

Jack found the last carriage door was too stiff to open, leaving him with no way out and no way back. He frantically rattled the door but it wouldn't budge. As the Trolls closed in, his last option, other than fighting (which didn't even occur to him as an option), was to curl up and hide between the last row of seats, head covered.

By now, the Trolls were in the carriage and approaching, their hushed voices sending shivers down his spine.

"He's in here, go round the end." one of them whispered.

Jack tightened his protective ball, as if shrinking could protect him from harm, and braced himself for the inevitable blow.

CRASH! BANG! YELP! A symphony of chaos

erupted in the carriage, the clash of bodies and smashing of glass rang out as the carriage rocked. Yet somehow, Jack remained uninvolved, his head hidden beneath his hands. Words of rage and cries of pain filled the musty air as the brawl continued, then just as quickly as it had all started, there was silence.

Footsteps slowly approached Jack, who still trembled beneath the seats, his head covered, prepared for a beating.

THUD! The pointed tip of an umbrella came down hard on the floor in front of him. Jack half opened one eye, stealing a look through his fingers. A tall, dark-skinned, muscular man in his late fifties crouched down and tilted his head to address him.

"You must be Jack."

Jack gingerly uncovered his face to look up.

"Sam? You have a deceptive phone voice…"

He offered Jack his hand and helped him up.

"Oswald. Come with me."

6th November, 0815hrs

Oswald led Jack along the tracks of an underground tunnel; more piles of embers provided a slight glow along the way, but Oswald didn't need them.

"I see you met the Trolls then?" Oswald was vaguely amused.

"Yeah, they're charming, aren't they? Do you live down here too then?"

"Not officially…"

Oswald stopped at a heavy iron door set into the wall of a tunnel, tapped a code into a keypad, and used his considerable weight to turn a metal wheel. The door screeched as it opened into a bunker, essentially a narrow tunnel filled with filing cabinets and office chairs. The walls were covered in newspaper clippings, and rusty metal shelves were stacked with soldering irons, nuts and bolts, tweezers, and precision screwdrivers. Electrical cables bunched together with cable ties connected a series of lights, gadgets, and computers.

Sam sat at a desk watching the news report with her back to the entrance.

"Found him; he'd made some friends." Oswald announced.

Sam spun the chair to face Jack, extending her

hand to shake.

"I'm Sam, hi."

Jack smiled, took her hand, and leaned forward to kiss it, in the manner of an old-timey gentleman. Sam recoiled, her head moving back and her brow furrowing. Jack held on to her hand, but at the last moment kissed the back of his own hand.

"The pleasure's all yours," he smirked, considering himself charming in an off-beat and original way. Sam tutted.

"Easy, Casanova," interjected Oswald.

"Sorry, are you two…?" Jack looked surprised.

"She's my daughter!"

Jack was relieved. "Excellent."

Jack winked at Sam, who frowned and looked away, unimpressed by his charms now she met him in real life. Oswald paused for a moment, internally questioning whether this was really the man they needed, then spoke: "We need your help."

"Yeah right, so I'm told. With what?"

Sam stepped in: "We don't exactly know, just that it was worth killing for and it's going to happen at about noon today."

"Everything's on the USB stick. Did you bring yours?" Oswald continued, holding up a thumb drive.

Jack held up his: "Yeah, not that useful as I remember…"

"I told you to turn off the WIFI," Sam interjected.

"Yeah right, OK." Jack grunted.

"If you'd followed my instructions properly, you'd have seen for yourself," said Sam, "We think the explosions last night were caused by something called FLEM."

"Phlegm? You'd need a bad cold to sneeze that hard." Jack quipped.

Sam did not find his joking funny; this was serious. Sensing an argument brewing, Oswald picked up the thread:

"FLEM's more likely to be an acronym, F-L-E-M. Fracking… something something, Mining, something like that. They weren't bombs last night; they were sinkholes caused by an earthquake."

It was Jack's turn to be unamused.

"Look, if you've pulled me down here for some daft conspiracy theory…"

"It's true, I was there, I heard them talking about it. And that earthquake caused the release of something called Pandora, which is going to be a massive problem."

"OK, and Pandora is…?"

"That's what we need to find out. From the level of encryption on the files, they're definitely hiding something big," said Oswald.

"Ha - that's what she said." Jack couldn't resist.

Sam tutted and frowned at Jack in disgust. "Oh, please!"

Jack was indignant. "That is what you said! 'Something big'."

"That is not what you meant. Have I really got to put up with…?"

Sam noticed Oswald's glare and stopped talking. He turned back to the computer and opened a file, clicking through page after page, occasionally stopping to type. Amidst the corrupted data, there were two files: "PHOENIX PROTOCOL" and "F.L.E.M."

"This is as far as I can get," said Oswald, turning the screen towards Jack.

He double-clicked the PHOENIX PROTOCOL file to show nine new folders, labelled "ALTERNATIVES 1 – 9". Jack looked at Oswald, then Sam, then back to Oswald. Finally, he raised his hands to shoulder level, palms up, and shrugged, still wondering what any of this had to do with him.

"These files use proximity-based security. That's

top-level secrecy," continued Oswald, ignoring Jack's apparent apathy.

"It means they'll only open if you have a special chip in your arm," translated Sam.

"Chip in your arm? Who has? To be honest, I think you've got the wrong man. We've got nothing to go on here; it's not a story. You don't know what has or will happen, who's done it, or when it will be. Plus, you may not have noticed, but I've already got a massive story on the wall. This is going to work out just fine for me, without any help from you."

"Oh right, I get it. You're all about the narrative." Oswald was starting to lose his patience. "Terrorists are among us, close the borders and keep us safe? The government will have your back as long as you toe the line? DON'T YOU LIVE OUT THERE?"

"Look, I just report the facts. We all need to make a living."

"Really? The facts?" Oswald was becoming increasingly animated by Jack's attitude. "I'll give you facts. You remember the 5/11 attack?"

"I think you'll find it was me who broke the story, mate! That's kind of my thing…"

"Oh yeah, it was The Unheard, right?"

"Obviously." Jack rolled his eyes in Sam's direction.

"OK. Do you know what a false flag is?"

"Erm - I have got a 2:1 in Journalism, you know…"

Oswald leaned forward and calmed his voice.

"Years ago I was Head of Data Collection at Dynasty, which gave me access to every data stream imaginable. While I was monitoring this data, I found out they were behind a series of so-called terrorist attacks."

"The government? Nah, I don't buy it, the government couldn't organise a fight at a football match. This is pure-bred one hundred percent conspiracy theory, right there. I suppose it was the Jews, was it?"

"Not the government, big business: primarily Dynasty, but other companies are up to the same thing. The conspiracy theories you talk about were planted by the same people to muddy the water, make it impossible to tell what's true and what's nonsense."

Jack took a moment to consider this, aware that accepting this premise would mean he'd been a corporate tool for the best years of his career.

"Nah, I'm still not buying it. Dynasty is just another profit-hungry property magnate, why would they bother?"

"To manufacture wars and gain public support for them."

"Again, why? Terrorists are religious nutters; you can see why they'd do it. What's a big business got to gain?"

"What does big business usually want to gain? Wars are expensive: they'd sell both sides the weapons they needed on credit. Then, when the wars were done, the countries destroyed and left in debt, Dynasty would clean up: private security, building contracts, food production, travel infrastructure, communications networks: whole countries rebuilt for the benefit of corporate profit at a huge cost to human life. They found out what I knew and made sure I was in Parliament on the day of the attack. You want to talk about conspiracies? I'll tell you about conspiracies."

Jack was beginning to question his entire history but wasn't ready to give in to Oswald so easily. He'd made his career on this and didn't want to back down now:

"You, sir, are a nutter. Hiding down here in your underground lair. I don't like the landlords either, but you're taking this way too far."

"They're so much more than landlords. You name it, they own it – banks, prisons, construction, arms manufacture, armies, border controls, shipping companies, social media. The media. They hold data on everyone; they know what you buy, where you go, what you watch, what you can be convinced of. Their algorithms use that data and don't just predict what you'll buy, but also how you'll vote, if you'll break the law, what type of misinformation might change that. This isn't conspiracy theory, it's what we're living and it's been going on since the start of the century. They basically control the world and then tell us what to think of it."

Oswald sat back, his somewhat practised speech complete. Jack remained sceptical.

"C'mon, it's all a bit much, isn't it? I've heard all this before, usually from total nutters who think the Earth is flat and landlords are lizards that drink children's blood."

"Look," said Sam, dangling the USB stick. "If this turns out to be true, it's going to make your terrorist story look like the weather report. Don't you want to know what they're hiding on here?"

The White Room – Jack

Jack leaned back and put his arms behind his head, very much enjoying the fact that the chair moved effortlessly to accommodate him.

"Where did you get this chair from? I need one of these in my life. Is this what rich people are sitting on these days?"

"How did you feel about learning that your life's work was based on a lie?"

"Well, let's be clear, I can't say I was completely sold at that point. I hear people talking like this all the time, usually absolute freaks who think vaccines are designed to kill you or the Earth's flat. Their theories generally fall apart in seconds."

"Why didn't you walk away?"

Jack looked over his shoulder as if someone might be eavesdropping before leaning forward.

"Aftershocks. Me and Owen definitely felt aftershocks; that's not what a bomb would do. Also, Sam told me those Props would turn up and they did. I'm glad I didn't hang around for that. Anyway, she was right – I really did want to know what was hiding on that USB stick."

6th November, 0830hrs

Without getting up, Oswald wheeled his chair over to a large metal trunk, battered and covered in old flight stickers: flying was strictly for landlords these days, so it must have been ancient. The trunk was locked shut with a combination padlock, which Oswald hid from Jack as he opened it. Inside the box lay a treasure trove of old, homemade gadgets fashioned from repurposed vintage relics, a fair indication of Oswald's skills and resourcefulness.

A jumble of wires, mismatched components and faded casings interconnected in a haphazard manner, screaming of ingenuity and the lost art of make-do-and-mend. He rifled through the trunk until he eventually found two trucker caps. He wheeled back past Sam and Jack to his desk, opened up a tattered wallet of precision tools, selected a narrow solder, and started melting things into place. Working quickly, he fiddled with wires that were already attached to the peaks of the caps before turning round to show them the newly decorated caps, LED lights lining the peaks.

"Nice. Bit disco for me though," remarked Jack, as he took one and turned it slowly, examining it from all angles.

"Anti-Facial-Recognition Caps," Oswald explained, "they've got LED lights in the peak, makes your face look like a ball of light on CCTV."

"Great, so as long as everyone else looks like a ball of light you'll blend in perfectly."

Oswald angrily snatched the hat back from Jack, his patience rapidly wearing thin.

"Enough wisecracks, this is serious! Am I getting through to you? Do you understand what's going on here?"

Oswald was now on his feet, pointing down at Jack.

"Yes, I understand." Jack put his hands up in surrender and cowered ever so slightly.

"Good, because you seem to be treating it like some sort of a laugh." Oswald composed himself and sat down. "We don't need to blend in, we just need to be anonymous."

"OK, what's the plan? I need details," asked Jack.

Oswald turned the computer screen towards him to show a list of names next to thumbnail ID pictures.

"We're going to use their tech against them. This is a list of employees with clearance, I reckon Nile Warwick's our man."

He clicked on a thumbnail to bring up the picture of a handsome young man, listed as the Head of Marketing.

"This guy is perfect, senior enough to have access to all areas, unimportant enough that nobody really pays him much attention. We get him, we get access. Every morning he's driven to HQ in a driverless limo. That's our chance."

Oswald rummaged through the boxes and coffee cups on his desk before producing a gun-like device, similar to a vintage Super 8 camera but wrapped in copper coils, and attached to an external battery, the kind old petrol cars used to need.

"With this." Oswald displayed the gun proudly.

Jack took it and turned it over in his hands.

"OK, I give up."

"It's a handheld EMP – it fires an electromagnetic pulse that knocks out all electrical devices within a 50 metre radius. That means his car, CCTV, Sentries, mobile phone. Everything."

Oswald pushed the junk off his desk and spread out a tattered paper map, the city walls drawn in with a marker pen, and traced a route along the streets, finishing on a small road just within the walls, a hundred metres or so from Dynasty HQ.

"He'll arrive from here." Oswald pointed at a VIP entrance through the walls. He traced a finger along a road, taking a ninety-degree turn onto his arrival point. He stopped at a point just short of Dynasty HQ.

"We'll get him here. Once we've deployed the EMP, his car will stop and the CCTV will be out. We'll have a few minutes to grab him, pull him into the tunnels and grab the chip."

"I thought it was in his arm…"

"We'll chop it off!" Sam sounded a little too enthusiastic about this idea.

"Chop his arm off? What with, are you hiding a samurai sword back there?" asked Jack.

"We're not chopping any arms off," said Oswald, "The chip's just under the skin, we just need to make a small incision."

Oswald closed Warwick's profile page and opened a new one, this time showing a photo of Lawson.

"Above all else, we need to avoid him."

"Yeah, he looks like somebody I'd generally avoid. Any specific reason?" asked Jack.

"This is Lawson, Dynasty's Head of Security. For that, read enforcer, fixer, private army general, thug. He's bad. You see him, you let me know. And run. In fact, run first, then let me know."

"I can't see him getting down here…" said Jack nonchalantly.

Oswald was slightly taken aback by this:

"While we're getting the chip. He'll be on your tail in no time if you're not quick."

Jack looked at Sam and laughed in disbelief.

"Wait, you think I'm going?"

"You want the story don't you?" said Oswald.

"Erm, you called me. This is not my field. Not. At. All. No chance, mate. What if I get caught? I'm the guy getting the word out, if something happens to me it's game over. Sorry, but I'm the talent in this scenario…"

Sam balked at his response:

"Seriously? Did you really just call yourself the talent?"

"You were suggesting we chop a man's arm off a second ago! I'm sorry, good luck with your field operation or whatever - I'm good right here. You get the info, I'll do the broadcast."

Oswald was incredulous. "You think I'm leaving a reporter in here? Unsupervised?"

Jack was momentarily distracted, intrigued by what Oswald could mean, but quickly folded his arms and sat tight:

"That's the deal, take it or leave it."

It was Sam who spotted the flaw in his plan:

"But that means bringing the chip back here – it's too risky! What if they follow us into the tunnels?"

"She's right, we can't risk being followed," agreed Oswald. "If they find out about me, or the fact that

I've basically been living right below them for the last ten years, they'll stop at nothing to flush me out."

Jack stood firm, his cowardice winning the battle with his need for fame.

"OK, how about this? I'm going to need my team, I'm guessing our newsroom is no good after this morning... What if I arrange a meeting place with them so we can broadcast, you send the chip there by drone, and I'll go and meet it."

Sam sighed and turned to Oswald:

"I think he was right when he said we've got the wrong man. If 'man' is the correct term," she practically spat the word 'man', as she gave Jack the side-eye.

Oswald was already digging through the shelves, eventually opening up a wooden box to find a battered drone.

"Actually, that works. We can get the chip and send him to meet it: it saves time and that's a factor. Jack, head back the way we came in, you'll see a white box on the wall with 'Emergency' written in red, inside there's a phone that works down here. Call your people, get them ready."

"What, now?" said Jack, surprised by the urgency.

"Yes now, have you not been listening? We have about four hours to figure all this out and possibly stop it."

Oswald gave Jack an ancient radio walkie-talkie, briefly explaining how to use it.

"Keep this radio on, nobody monitors analogue comms. Keep it on channel 3, press this to talk, let go to listen. When you've finished speaking, say 'Over' and I'll know it's okay to press my button and reply."

Sam threw Jack a disappointed look as she put the cap on her head and the EMP into a backpack.

"Ready, Sam?" asked Oswald as he put his cap on.

"Ready. Let's go."

The White Room – Sam

"How did you feel about Jack at this point?"

"Disappointed. He was so arrogant. And entitled. I really thought we'd got the wrong person…"

"What would the right person have been like?"

"I don't know. Brave, I suppose. At least, braver than him. We were about to go up against a massive corporation, the same one that tried to kill my dad. I needed someone who was on the side of the people and prepared to take risks in order to help them."

"Do you think it was fair to ask so much of a stranger?"

"I mean, probably not, but this was not normal.

From what I'd seen, everyone was in danger. I needed someone who understood the severity of the situation."

"How did you feel about the situation?"

"Scared, I suppose. There was obviously something coming, but it could have been anything. My mum was at home, probably thinking I was still in bed. What was I supposed to tell her? I didn't want to warn her until I knew what I was warning her about… also, she'd have been worried sick about me running around underground, fighting landlords. Then there was the whole, Dad-not-really-being-dead thing…"

"Tell me about that. How did you feel about lying to your mother?"

Sam shifted her weight as the chair moulded around her, discomforted by the direction the discussion was taking.

"It was hard, but you have to understand my parents split up when I was about eight, they didn't really speak to each other much. I saw Dad on Saturdays for a few hours – not even every Saturday actually, he had this really important, intense job. Mum always said it was the reason they split up.

"When the police came to tell us he'd died in the attack on Parliament, Mum was distraught. I remember not really feeling very much about it. I was eleven at the time, I cried when I saw Mum crying but when I was alone, or in class at school, I wasn't thinking about how sad I was that he'd gone, I was wondering why I wasn't sad. That actually made me more upset than losing him, the fact I didn't feel anything about it. It was weird, I don't know what was going on there."

"How did you find out he was alive?"

"About a week after his funeral I found a walkie-talkie in my school bag, with a Post-it note saying to press the button. I pressed it and my dad's voice came on, telling me not to panic and not to tell anyone. This was straight after the attack, so all the tubes into London were stopped and he'd moved below ground. At first, he'd meet me in the park after school. When I was old enough to go out alone, I started meeting him underground. I had a way in through an alley in Shoreditch."

"Did it upset you to lie to your mother?"

"Of course, she was really upset when he died. I'm not sure she ever got over it actually."

"You weren't tempted to tell her?"

"So many times! Every time I found her crying in the kitchen. When I got older, I told myself she was crying because she was broke and single, but she wasn't actually that badly off, not compared to other people in the area. Dad had life insurance from his job, she was the beneficiary. It was enough to avoid living in the slums…"

6th November, 0845hrs

Sam stuck close to Oswald's side as they trekked through the eerie darkness of the damp, abandoned tunnel, their way lit by the LEDs in their caps. The air was thick with the musty scent of decay, occasional flickers of light casting strange, shifting shadows on the moss-covered walls.

She couldn't help but wonder about the history of this place. She had vague memories of travelling by tube, but when the walls went up, the trains had stopped and heavy-duty grills were installed, blocking access to the tunnels below central London.

The silence was oppressive, broken only by the occasional drip of water and the crunch of their boots. The sense of isolation seemed to seep from the walls, while perspective gave the impression that the tunnel would eventually close in on them, adding claustrophobia to her growing list of negative feelings.

The moisture in the air left a cool, clammy sensation on Sam's skin. She shivered and turned to Oswald:

"He's such a coward."

"Unfortunately, he's our only option," Oswald replied.

"I mean, I guess he's right, sort of… he's got millions of subscribers, what have we got?"

"It is what it is. I wish I didn't have to bring you into it though."

"I think you'll find I brought you into this, actually. Besides, I've got skills!"

Sam karate-chopped his arm and jabbed his leg. Oswald laughed and brushed her away, she kicked again before stepping in a deep, muddy puddle, covering her shoe up to her ankle.

"Ew!"

She freed her foot and squelched on, frowning, while Oswald picked up his walkie-talkie.

"Jack, we're nearly there, have you got that address for us yet? Over"

"I'm working on it," came the crackling reply.

"What's the magic word? Over."

"Is that a trick question?"

Oswald looked at Sam and sighed, this time holding his response.

"Is that a trick question? OVER," said Jack, providing the correct sentence.

"That's better and no it's not. Quickly with the address please. Over and out."

Oswald strapped the walkie-talkie to his chest and stopped beneath a rusted manhole cover. With a burst of energy, he leapt, fingers outstretched, to grab hold of a sturdy metal ladder that had been concealed in the shadows, hoisting it down to meet the ground with a subtle clank.

"You OK?" he asked Sam.

"Yep. Hey, do you think you and Mum would ever have got back together? You know, if you hadn't died?" She raised her fingers to enact air-quotes as she said the last word.

Oswald hesitated for a moment, one hand resting on the ladder, and gently placed his other hand on Sam's shoulder as he looked her in the eye.

"Is that really what's on your mind right now?"

"Well, you know, it was the anniversary of your death yesterday, she misses you."

"Who knows? Maybe." Oswald pondered, his voice tinged with nostalgia. "I don't remember us getting on all that well by the end…"

"It's not too late though, is it? You could tell her."

Oswald offered a fleeting, melancholic smile.

"I think ten years is probably the cut-off point for admitting you're not really dead, isn't it? Let's focus on this for now, yeah?"

Oswald began climbing the ladder, Sam following closely behind. At the top, he deftly put one leg through the rungs, allowing him to lean backwards and use both hands to slowly lift the manhole cover from its place, gently sliding it to the side with a grace at odds with the harsh scraping sound it produced. Peering out into the street above, he was relieved to find the street deserted.

Oswald checked in all directions and cautiously climbed out of the tunnel onto the street, staying low as he reached down to help Sam up. She emerged beside him, recognising a collection of luxury services, bars and restaurants known as Spitalfields, most of which were shuttered and silent so early in the day.

"It looks like people are taking the threat seriously," she pointed out. "Should we be worried about that? I really don't want to get bombed."

"It won't happen," said Oswald, reassuringly. "It's just a distraction. They clearly want people out of the way today."

Spotting a cluster of CCTV cameras, Oswald took Sam's arm and hurriedly pulled her into an alleyway behind the old market. Slow-moving traffic could be seen in the distance, towards the banks, with Props at various checkpoints along the way.

"We're never going to spot Warwick in time from here. We need to be higher up."

"How about there?" Sam pointed out a high-rise car park overlooking the street.

"Perfect."

Staying low and near the buildings, they scurried to the car park, slipping through a pedestrian entrance into the brutal concrete monolith. Rapidly ascending a flight of echoing stairs, they felt the chill of the cold, hard concrete as they made their way to the first floor. There were no cars inside; the few workers that still owned cars were no longer allowed to drive inside the walls as the checks took too long and cars could be ramming devices. The Landlords were ferried around in driverless cars, some of which returned to car parks overnight.

Quickly they found a vantage point; obscured from cameras, providing a view of the street below, with Dynasty HQ's main entrance a hundred metres further along. They positioned themselves for the intercept, Sam keeping half an eye on the office building, its lifts whizzing up and down the exterior while Props remained a motionless presence. Oswald quickly set up his gadgets.

"We don't have long, he should be here any minute," Oswald exclaimed urgently, beads of sweat forming on his forehead as he frantically connected a web of cables to his battered laptop.

"What if he doesn't come to work today? He might be scared of the attack too."

"Unlikely, given that the threat isn't real. Even if it is, Dynasty is very well defended. First, the sentries on the wall are programmed to target anything trying to pass over them. Then if one did somehow sneak through, Dynasty has their own set of guns on the roof."

He connected a phone and a pair of binoculars to the laptop and typed in his password, tapping his fingers impatiently as he waited for the ping that would signal a successful connection. Handing Sam the binoculars he pointed away from Dynasty.

"Keep the binoculars facing cars coming from that direction."

The left-hand side of his computer screen showed the binoculars' point of view. Traffic was gradually building up, a few cars had turned into the road and were heading towards them slowly. As they approached, the binoculars targeted each car, transcribing information – registration plate, car ownership details, outstanding fines, and anything else a police database might hold.

The rest of the screen was running facial recognition software as faces became visible, scrolling through a list of Dynasty employees' names in search of matches. The data on the screen changed rapidly, but Sam wasn't paying too much attention, she was focused on the street.

Eventually, the device beeped and a red square highlighted an oncoming limousine. The binoculars zoomed in to show the passenger was the man from the profile pictures.

'NILES WARWICK – MATCH'

Oswald looked up from the screen.

"That's him, are you ready?"

"As ready as I'll ever be…"

Oswald quickly packed up, rushing to get everything in his backpack, before leading Sam back out into the street and taking shelter in the doorway of a closed restaurant.

Reaching back into his bag, Oswald pulled out the EMP and rested his thumb on the trigger, aiming it towards the car like a mobile speed camera.

"OK, set the timer to three minutes."

Sam took a clockwork egg timer from her pocket and turned the dial to three. The car they needed was still a little way off in traffic as Oswald counted down:

"Three…"

Cars passed by, one by one. Warwick was waiting at traffic lights, no other cars behind him.

"Two…"

As the traffic lights changed, Warwick's limo glided towards them, the last in a steady flow of driverless executive vehicles. Oswald hesitated for a moment, to avoid stopping any other cars.

"ONE!"

He pulled the EMP's trigger and Sam started the timer. As he did so, the limousine started to slow down, silently coasting along before gently bumping into a street light, in the dullest car crash of all time.

"Is that it?" Sam asked, slightly disappointed.

"What did you expect, explosions?"

Oswald sprinted to the lifeless vehicle, his footsteps suddenly pounding in the silence of a power-free area. Nestled in the back seat, he found Warwick, his disoriented countenance a sharp contrast to the handsome young man in the photographs. This man was much older and extremely overweight, a stark disparity from his digital profile.

In the confined space of the car's interior, Warwick appeared lost and bewildered. With the car doors' usual automatic function now out of action, he could only gaze at Oswald, whom he assumed had approached out of genuine concern.

"Oh thank you! I don't know what…" Warwick began through the window, his muffled words cut short as Oswald violently rammed a crowbar into the side of the door, tearing it open. In one swift and ruthless motion, Oswald seized Warwick by the shirt, pulling him forcibly towards the door.

Before he had time to realise what was happening, Oswald had landed a brutal head-butt with a thud to the top of Warwick's nose. Blood spurted in all directions as Warwick was knocked unconscious and crumpled back into the car. Faced with the dead weight of his enormous frame, Oswald struggled to pull him from the car.

"30 seconds down!" warned Sam.

"He's way bigger than I thought," Oswald panted, "I don't think he'll fit through the manhole."

"Bloody dishonest profile pics, story of my life…" muttered Sam, "What now?"

Oswald scanned his surroundings in search of a solution, a glimmer of desperation in his eyes. Quickly he landed on a small massage shop nestled in amongst the nail bars and hair salons of Spitalfields. A small Asian woman was just unlocking the doors as they hauled a slowly stirring Warwick towards it, like a big game hunter's prize. The petite masseuse let out a shrill cry as Oswald pushed her through the door to force his way in, pointing aggressively at her, then at the corner of the room.

"QUIET! Stay where you are." he hissed at her, his imposing physique enough to make most people cooperate with his demands, his eyes suggesting a terrible fate if she did not.

She screamed again as he hoisted Warwick's limp body onto the massage table.

"QUIET!"

Warwick started to come round; confused and in pain as he touched his nose, alarmed by the blood he found smeared across his fingers. Oswald did not hesitate to deliver another punishing blow, leading the masseuse to scream out once more.

"Two minutes left," Sam cautioned, not sure of the best way to help this sudden change of plan.

Oswald rolled Warwick over on the table, exposing the wrist where a small scar indicated the insertion of a microchip. His fingers traced over the blemish, searching for the telltale lump beneath the skin. Satisfied that he'd found it, he took a craft knife and cut into Warwick's flesh with a determined hand.

Feeling of little use, Sam picked up the radio and called Jack.

"Jack, are you working on a meeting place? Over."

Only a slight crackle came in response. She tried again:

"JACK! WHAT'S HAPPENING? OVER."

This time came an immediate reply:

"I can't figure out this phone – there's no screen, just a circle of plastic with numbers round it. I tried pressing the numbers but nothing happens."

Overhearing this, Oswald stepped in:

"It's a dial phone, put your finger in the hole where the number is and push the circle around, clockwise, until your finger can't turn anymore. Then let it reset and do the same with the next number. Do you understand? Over?"

"Got it." Jack gingerly fingered the dial, pushing the zero around to the stopper. He lifted his finger out and jumped as the dial returned to its original position.

"This is mad," he muttered to himself, "What's wrong with having a screen?"

In the massage booth, Sam continued her countdown:

"Ninety seconds."

Oswald deftly manipulated Warwick's skin, pushing flesh and squeezing on tweezers. "I think I've got it."

He fiddled for a moment more and then produced a small, blood-covered cartridge from the man's arm.

The masseuse screamed again, cowering in the corner, aghast at the situation.

"That's it!" called Oswald, "Let's go!"

Sam called Jack again:

"Jack, we need that address! Over!"

"On it!" came a hurried reply.

Down below, Jack crouched below the phone, waiting for an answer, unsure if it was even possible to connect to a modern phone from an ancient contraption like this. Eventually, the ring tone stopped and Bill's weary voice answered, cautious at the unknown number:

"Hello?"

"Hello, Bill? It's me. Are you in work yet?"

"Jack, why the weird number? I'm just about to leave, congrat…"

Jack cut him short:

"Good, don't go, we've got trouble. Listen, have you still got friends at the BBC?"

In the massage parlour, as Warwick groaned and shifted on the table, Oswald loaded the drone with the chip and USB stick. All four occupants were struggling with their own fears, whether for themselves or for others, the tension was palpable as they all knew things would get much worse if they were interrupted. Sam smiled at the frightened masseuse, gently attempting to soothe her frayed nerves and avoid her alerting the outside world to their exploits. She raised a hand to the masseuse's arm to comfort her, but she recoiled quickly, fearing she would also be attacked. Sam decided to leave her be but felt terrible for scaring her so badly.

Once the drone was loaded up, Oswald took the walkie-talkie, urgently in need of a destination:

"Talk to me, Jack. Over."

"OK, are you ready? You're sending it to BBC Television Centre, W12 7RJ."

"Are you having a laugh? That place has been derelict for years, isn't it full of squatters? Over."

"Trust me, it's our best bet."

Oswald typed the address into his laptop and waited as it calculated a route, immediately unplugging the cable when the calculation was complete.

"OK, go now - the drone's on its way. Over and out."

As they burst through the door and rushed out into the open air, Sam threw the drone skyward, its propellers springing into action automatically as it set off towards the old broadcasting centre.

Their pace was charged with urgency as they made for the manhole cover, but a sight ahead stopped them in their tracks. A line of armoured cars was streaming out of Dynasty HQ, heading directly for them. Oswald put his arm out to stop Sam, nodding towards the advancing threat. Spotting a row of spotlessly clean rubbish bins to the side of the road, they sought refuge, concealing themselves from the view of passing cars.

"Stay low," whispered Oswald, "It looks like they're onto us."

They watched through the gaps in the bins as the Props drove past, then screeched to a halt thirty metres along the road. With the manhole in the middle of the road, halfway between them and the guards, they were stuck.

"Now what?" asked Sam, the edge in her voice suggesting that the seriousness of the situation had hit her.

"For the moment we wait here. There'll be more coming." Oswald remained cautious but calm.

As the Props poured out into the street, Oswald and Sam moved around the bins, crouching to remain out of sight. They waited with bated breath, acutely aware that if Props came their way, it was all over.

An officer barked a series of rapid-fire instructions which appeared to give the Props a sense of purpose, and as a well-coordinated unit, they stormed the car park.

"They think we're still in there. We need to go. Now!"

As the Props disappeared from view, they made a break for the manhole cover. Oswald heaved the cover open as they arrived, extending his hand out to Sam.

"You first, quick."

As Sam's head dropped below road level, the door of the massage parlour swung open and a blood-smeared Warwick staggered out. Spotting his assailant about to escape, he started shouting at the top of his voice.

"Help! Guards, that's the one! He's out here!"

A single Prop poked his head over the first-floor barrier to investigate, as Warwick frantically waved and pointed, a handkerchief pressed to his flattened nose.

"That way! They're getting away!"

With that, power returned and CCTV cameras came back to life, quickly panning in every direction before zeroing in on their prey. The Props shifted direction with remarkable speed, a frenzy of shouted instructions and the arrival of additional vehicles, adding to the pandemonium.

As Oswald pulled the manhole cover over him and dropped down into the tunnel, the shouting was only slightly muffled.

"Did they see us?" asked Sam, anxiety etched on her face as her nerves started to get the better of her.

"Don't worry about it, just run."

They sprinted down the dark, dank tunnel, their footsteps echoing along the desolate passage. Despite needing to slow down, Sam couldn't resist turning back to check for pursuing Props. She could see torches flashing from the manhole, but the Props were not following them down into the tunnels.

"Dad! DAD!"

"Keep moving!"

"No, Dad - they're not following."

Oswald stopped to see for himself, his curiosity getting the better of him.

"That is odd…"

"Maybe they're trying to cut us off."

"No, some would still follow."

Their hurried pace continued but with less haste: half running, half walking, all the while unease growing at what they might find ahead.

As they approached the first turn, Sam felt a small shower of grit land in her hair. She pointed her torch up to the overhead arches as more fell, the floor began to vibrate, growing in intensity as a deep, ominous crunching sound reverberated through the tunnel. A crack formed in the adjacent wall, allowing more grit, soil, and bricks to cascade to the ground.

"Dad! We need to get out of here!" urged Sam.

"Not yet, cameras will pick us up straight away. Our exit's just a bit further."

"But what if this is the earthquake starting?"

"No," said Oswald, checking his watch, "It's only nine o'clock – too early."

"The wall then? They said they'd attack the walls!"

"Then we're safer down here. It's just a tremor, don't worry."

Oswald spoke with confidence, but he knew the potential danger they faced by staying underground. He grappled with the weight of the situation, the risk he had imposed on Sam, the danger of the unknown: he hated himself for it, but he didn't want to scare her. Either way, leaving the tunnels inside the walls would be pointless, they'd be picked up immediately. Better to gamble for freedom.

6th November, 0900hrs

Jack's heart raced, pumping cortisol through his veins as the latest tremor rattled his senses. Having completed his part of the mission, he was navigating his way back to Oswald's bunker, and the tremors were making the tunnel's ceiling groan and fracture, filling the air with dust and foreboding. Jack fumbled nervously to free the walkie-talkie from his pocket, pawing clumsily at the buttons as he called to Oswald for help.

"Oswald? Oswald? Are you there…? Are you there, over?"

"I'm here, over," came a crackling reply.

"Did you feel that? Has the attack started?"

"I don't know." Oswald was not so concerned about scaring Jack.

"Well, am I better off down here or outside? The roof's cracking, I don't want to get buried."

"Just stick to the plan, I'll—"

The walkie-talkie started to deteriorate, rapidly devolving into white noise. Jack weighed up his options; turn left and he'd be back towards Old Shoreditch station. He knew he could get out that way, but he risked running into Trolls. Turn right and he'd be back at Oswald's den, but he risked being buried alive.

An ear-splitting screech of metal grating against stone made his mind up for him; if the Trolls had any sense, they'd be leaving too. He tried again to make contact:

"Oswald?"

Jack shook the walkie-talkie desperately, stabbing at the buttons and turning the dial, but he heard only a disheartening wall of static. With stoic determination, he carefully felt his way along the cold, grimy tiles, retracing his path to the station platform from which he'd fallen earlier. As the ground intermittently trembled below him, damage to the walls around him built up, distant cracks conjoined, and loosened bricks fell. He dashed through a short tunnel and reached the defunct escalator just in time to avoid a mess of rubble and cables as a section of the ceiling collapsed.

He bounded up the stairs, leaping three steps at a time and sped towards the boarded-up exit, smashing through the rusty sheet of corrugated iron to clear his path from the station. Squeezing through the gap, he twisted and turned to land flat on his back in the street on the other side. He was scratched and bruised but relieved to have avoided an early burial. He delved deep into his pocket in search of his keys and scanned the area for his bike. To his initial confusion and subsequent anger, all he found was a frame.

"Oh for f... Thank you. THANK YOU,

LONDON, that's perfect. Today, of all days!"

Jack felt a buzz against his leg as his phone started to ring. With a quick rummage, he pulled out the phone and fumbled, dropping it on the ground. He could see the screen showed 'NAN' calling. A sudden surge of guilt washed over Jack as he realised he hadn't told her he'd be staying out with all this going on. He quickly accepted the call.

"Nan! Morning."

"Jack! Where've you been? I've been trying to call you all morning, I've been worried sick!"

"Yep, I know, my bad. I Harked though, I thought you'd see it."

"What do you mean you Harked? You know I don't use that rubbish. What's wrong with a text?"

"I know, Nan, I'm sorry. Is the house alright? Anything damaged?"

"Damaged? What are you on about? Why would it be damaged?"

"The earthquake!"

"Earthquake? What earthquake? I haven't heard about an earthquake?"

"Last night, it's caused chaos. Haven't you seen the news? Or been outside?"

"I've only been up for ten minutes. I was just bringing you a cup of tea, and you weren't there, so I got worried."

"OK, well there was a big one last night, it's pretty serious—big holes in the roads, the pub went into a sinkhole!"

"There was a big dangerous earthquake last night and you're only checking in on me now? What if our house had sunk into the ground? What would you have done then?"

She had a point. Jack had seen some terrible things over the last few hours. The idea of his nan trapped under a girder made him shudder.

"I know, I'm really sorry. You wouldn't believe how hectic it's been. Are you okay though?"

"Well, of course, I'm okay. Don't you think I'd have started with that if I wasn't? That's no excuse though, you should have called! Why didn't you?"

"It was late, then I was underground, no signal."

"Underground? What do you mean, underground? You can't go underground anymore."

"Yeah, I kind of got caught up in a story. It made the walls, did you see?"

"Walls, my arse... you can't scare me like that. Not at my age... Listen, I've got real eggs for dinner. You'll be back by then, will you?"

"Yes, I'll be back. Sorry for worrying you. I've got to go though, I'm working on something big."

"Oh yeah, I've heard that one before. Is it about the earthquake?"

Jack didn't know whether or not to warn his nan about the looming disaster. He didn't want to scare her, or set her off telling everyone else. On the other hand, he would never forgive himself if she was harmed due to his omission.

"Sort of. Listen, Nan, everything's going to be fine. I'll see you later."

"OK, love, if you say so. You'll be home for six?"

"Yep, love you, bye!"

Jack hung up and started jogging, keen to find a quicker way to get to White City, trying to put aside the guilt from upsetting his nan.

6th November, 0915hrs

Oswald continued to lead the way as they rushed back to his den, his familiarity indispensable in these dimly lit tunnels.

"I don't think they're following," said Sam, slowing and falling back to check behind her.

"Don't think, just move." Oswald did not break his pace.

As they pressed forward, a deafening CRACK from above engulfed the tunnel, and the ceiling fractured. A pipe burst, sending a torrent of scalding steam hissing between them and throwing Sam to the floor. Oswald stopped in his tracks and turned back, his view obscured by the steam.

"SAM!"

With a loud CRUNCH, a heap of rubble tumbled down from the ceiling, completely blocking the tunnel and separating them from one another. Oswald rushed toward the debris, hoping to find Sam, but it was clear that the path was blocked by colossal chunks of stone and twisted, immovable iron bars.

"Sam! Sam, are you OK?"

Sam's reply was muffled by the sudden barrier.

"I'm alright! I can't see a way through though. What should I do?"

"First of all, stay calm. You need to go back and get above ground. Use the entrance behind Shoreditch High Street. You're gonna have to use your pass to get outside the walls!"

"But…"

"You'll have to risk it. I'm going to go the other way and meet you there. I'm sorry, Sam, I can't see another way. Keep your hat on, at least facial recognition won't pick you up!"

"OK, see you in a bit…"

Sam started jogging back, her LED cap providing the sole source of light. Fumbling her way through the inky darkness, she searched for an alternative way out, wondering what had happened to the glowing embers that usually lit the way. As she proceeded, the soft squelching around her feet developed into the distinct sound of splashing. She stopped to investigate, holding the LED lights to the floor. Water was pooling around her feet and appeared to be flowing slightly. A distant rushing noise grew louder, and Sam's eyes widened in realisation.

"Shit!"

She looked up as the little light around her bounced off a knee-high wave hurtling towards her. Bracing herself, she clung to the pipes that ran along the tunnel walls to avoid being knocked off her feet once more. Pushing against the rising tide, she kept going in search of the exit she needed.

The water was rapidly rising, and the current was getting stronger as it reached her waist. Realising she would not make the exit she was looking for, she started to panic, willing to try anything to escape the oncoming tsunami.

A recess in the tiles provided hope; an emergency exit! Locating the push bar well below the water line, she pushed to open the door, but it didn't shift. Like most ways in and out of the underground tunnels, it was boarded up from the outside. With water lapping at her chest, she strained against the door, hoping against hope to find the strength to push through. But the door stood firm; clearly, her strength alone would not be enough.

Taking a deep breath, she ducked down below the water, clinging to the door with one hand as she scrabbled around in search of a tool to aid her escape, struggling against the ever-growing current. Her fingers closed around a piece of rebar, freed by the tremors, providing her only hope of escape. Still holding her breath underwater, she tried to find a gap in the frame where she could stick the metal bar, something to provide the leverage she needed. Finding no such respite, she surfaced, gasping for air, realising that the tunnel was now almost completely flooded.

Desperation fuelled her efforts as she pounded the door with the rebar, screaming for help. With the tunnel now nearly submerged, she took a final breath and ducked once more. Trying to stay calm, she finally found a gap in the doorframe, into which she rammed the rebar. With her back against the door, her feet searched the floor, finding purchase in a reassuringly solid crack in the ground. Summoning all her strength in a last bid to survive, she pushed on the rebar and forced her shoulders into the door. With the combination of her pushing and the weight of the water, the door buckled with a crunch, swinging open into a small stairwell.

Sam spilled out with the swell, her head smacking hard against a step as she fell, knocking her out cold. The rushing water quickly filled the stairwell, lifting Sam to street level and depositing her at the top of the steps as the water subsided. As she lay unconscious, a solitary CCTV camera swivelled and looked down, pointing directly at her exposed face.

6th November, 0930

Emerging from the manhole, Oswald found himself in a surreal landscape that bore the scars of the recent tremors. Unlike the buildings inside the walls, many out here were shoddy DIY structures that were shaky at the best of times. Even those that were built properly were now so old that the mortar had lost its integrity, allowing bricks and cornices to fall to the ground, smashing through shacks below. The resulting collapses made the area resemble a war zone. Fire billowed from the windows of buildings, casting a menacing, dancing shadow on the city walls. Large fissures snaked across the roads, joining the potholes as if completing an invisible artwork, and water spewed from ruptured drains.

Amid the chaos, a group of men were running a voluntary rescue operation, pulling people and belongings from crushed pre-fabs. At the roadside, a forlorn child sat on the curb, her tearful cries echoing the distress of countless others, her tiny hands clutching a charred and dishevelled teddy bear. The services one would expect in such circumstances were notable only for their absence, tied up as they were, attending to the minor problems the landlords were dealing with inside the walls.

Oswald's gaze shifted up to the towering walls

where the screens showed the Prime Minister, a stern and resolute woman in her late 50s, addressing a sombre press conference.

"Last night's horrific attacks serve only to strengthen our resolve. We will not bow to terrorism. If you perpetrated this act, we will find you. If you know who perpetrated this act, we will find you. If you support acts of this type, we will find you. I give you my word as Prime Minister that we will stop at nothing to keep this country safe from those that wish us harm."

Oswald was distracted by the HONK! HONK! of a van out of control, careening straight for him as it swerved to avoid crashing into a pile of rubble. In a heart-stopping moment, the van turned hard, causing it to topple over, forcing Oswald to dive to the ground and out of its path. Landing flat on his face, Oswald lay with his arms covering his head, braced for impact. The van skidded to a halt alongside him, filling the air with debris and adding to the chaos.

As the dust settled and danger subsided, Oswald cautiously rolled over and sat up, momentarily calm amid the tumultuous scene. With disarray stretching in every direction, he took in the sight and took a moment to think about Sam, aware that he had no way of contacting her to check she'd escaped the tunnels. With a sigh, he reached for his walkie-talkie.

Meanwhile, Jack was also outside the walls, navigating the post-tremor pandemonium and wondering how a tremor had caused so much destruction. He jogged across Old Street roundabout, hoping that the monorail to White City would still be operational. As one of the few working public amenities outside the walls, the monorail provided a valuable lifeline, not just for transportation but for the rare panoramic views it provided of outer London, sitting high above the buildings as it did. It whisked passengers along the outer edges of what had once been Zone 1, stopping at regular intervals to allow workers access to the wall's trade entrances.

With carnage surrounding him, Jack was unable to resist his journalistic tendencies. Honing in on a particularly expansive crack in the road, he pulled out his phone to film it. He followed the edge of the crevice until he found a car swallowed whole, the doors pinned shut by the jagged concrete. With his camera rolling, Jack got onto his belly and looked down into the car, camera first.

Inside, a man was beating on the window, unable to find a way out. Jack leaned in with the camera, but before he could say anything, he was interrupted by the crackle of the radio.

"JACK! JACK! IT'S OSWALD. ARE YOU THERE? OVER!"

Jack ignored the radio, crouching lower to get a

better shot of the trapped man, before crawling over the edge of the hole and getting his camera up to the windscreen.

"What's your name?" he asked the driver.

"Help me!" came the incredulous reply.

Jack leaned in further, his head now below ground level.

"What's that? Can you speak up a bit? It's for the news."

A loud crunch was swiftly followed by a shower of dust, bouncing off the roof of the car and getting in Jack's hair. The radio hissed again.

"JACK! OVER!"

This time he reacted, getting off the ground to stand up and dust off the grit before removing the walkie-talkie from his belt. Turning his back on his unfortunate interviewee, he walked away from the crash to respond.

"Oswald. I'm just in the middle of interviewing a survivor! This is gold dust…"

A thunderous CRASH shook the ground, prompting Jack to lunge forward, twisting as he did so, to locate the cause of the commotion. A huge section of the building had collapsed and now occupied the exact spot where the car (and Jack) had been just a second ago, leaving nothing more than a tailpipe as grim evidence.

Jack stood in stunned silence for a moment, the radio pressed to his chest, as reality set in: he had just witnessed a man's tragic death, very narrowly avoiding the same fate himself. He wrestled for a moment with the urge to inspect further, but fearful of what he might see, he decided to back away. He raised the radio without looking away from the disaster before him.

"Erm… Never mind. How's it going?" Jack continued, more subdued than he had been.

"Not great. They flooded the underground." Oswald's voice was broken as he responded, although this was disguised as the radio cracked and hissed.

"What? Flooded the underground? How? Who? The Unheard?" Jack's voice was laced with bewilderment.

"I don't know. It wasn't an attack on the walls though—this was in the tunnels."

"You're kidding, right? It couldn't have been the earthquake?"

"I don't know, it's too much of a coincidence; the Props saw us but didn't follow us into the tunnels, like they knew what was coming."

"What about Sam?"

"We got separated, I've not heard from her yet. Hopefully we'll meet up later. Where are you now?"

"On my way to the Beeb, on foot. Some twat had my bike. Most of it anyway."

"We don't have much time... I'll get there as soon as I can."

"OK. I'm right by the monorail, I'll give that a go. Over and out."

Jack was relieved to find the monorail was still operational, although as a relatively modern structure, it was not surprising it had easily weathered the storm. He sprinted up the stairs to the platform, high above the city streets, and waited for a train, all the while grappling with the weight of the tragedy he had just avoided.

6th November, 0945hrs

Jack took a seat at the front of the driverless train as it slipped above the slums below. He'd always enjoyed sitting in that seat, with its three-way view, and still considered any other seat a disappointment. He thought back to his youth, when the train was new, and remembered his Nan treating him to a ride the whole way round, getting off at the same stop they'd started from. He'd sat in the same seat then, pretending he was driving the train, as his Nan had pointed out important places like the old Palace, from when England had a King, and the Tower of London, where they'd kept all his stolen jewels.

That had been before the wall went up; nothing of interest was visible anymore, just the wall and its rolling mix of news and advertising to his left, and the broken remnants of London to his right.

He didn't really remember that much about the times before the wall; he'd only been in his early teens at the time of the attack. What he did know, he'd got from his Nan, who often spoke about a time when there was free healthcare, ordinary people owned houses, and everyone, not just the landlords, got to vote in elections. It seemed so unlikely, he'd always assumed she was applying some sort of filter to her memories. After all, if all that had been real, how could people have allowed such a change to happen?

Thirty feet below, people were on the streets trying to repair their makeshift homes, put out fires, and bail out floods. As the train leaned into a gentle curve, the old BBC centre could just be seen in the distance, its huge crescent barely visible beneath the ivy and overgrown grass that covered most of its facade, the perfect camouflage for a pirate news station. Jack picked up his radio and called for Oswald.

"Oswald, are you there? Over?"

"I'm here. Where are you? Over," came Oswald's breathless response.

"I'm just coming up on White City now."

"OK, get in touch with your guys, they should have the USB by now. I'm going to find Sam. Over and out."

"OK, keep in touch."

Jack took out his phone and brushed the screen with his thumb, selecting Bill from the recent video calls list. Before the first ring had rung, Bill's haggard face appeared on the screen, brimming with nervous energy despite his lack of sleep.

"Morning, Bill. Howzit?" enquired Jack.

"You mean aside from the collapsing ceilings?"

"What, where you are?"

"Yeah, it's a pretty old building… I think it'll hold up though."

"OK, well that's something, I suppose. Did you get everything?"

"Yeah, I think so, we're just loading up now. Listen, how did you get all this? Why couldn't we go to the office?"

"That's a long story, I'll fill you in when I get there. Listen, make sure you turn WIFI off before you open any files, that's important."

Bill nodded rather than answering, setting his phone upright so that he could type as he talked. Jack allowed him to fiddle for a moment before interrupting.

"You got anything?"

Bill nodded again, his brow furrowing deeper as he clicked open various files.

"We've got a bunch of folders labelled Alternatives 1-9 and one called Phoenix Protocol. Does that mean anything to you?"

"Yep, I got that far. Can you open them?"

"Trying now."

Jack waited for something new, searching for clues to their contents from Bill's reactions.

"And?"

"Yep, it's working… there's loads of new files

opening up, we need to narrow it down. What exactly are we looking for?"

Jack's impatience started to show.

"I don't know, start clicking!"

As Bill opened more files, a small crowd of coworkers surrounded him, looking over his shoulder with increasing interest. Annoyed to be left out, Jack called out.

"Oi, can you put the phone where I can see it, please?"

Bill handed the phone to his assistant, Becky, who pointed the camera at the computer screen as Bill started clicking open files, starting with a folder named "ALTERNATIVE 1". Within this folder were a number of files, each with indexed names that appeared to be random letters and numbers. The first picture showed a large, metallic chamber with a circular glass window on one side. Through the foggy glass, a faint outline of a human figure could be seen, encased in ice. The chamber was surrounded by an array of blinking lights and monitors displaying various temperatures and pressure readings.

"Can you see this?" asked Bill.

"More or less," replied Jack, squinting in an attempt to get a clear view.

Bill clicked on the next image, a series of vials filled with a bright green liquid. The vials were neatly arranged in a rack, each labelled with a sequence of alphanumeric codes. Beside them, a pair of gloved hands held a syringe, about to extract some of the liquid.

Bill clicked through to a picture of a large room filled with several upright cylindrical pods, each with a transparent front. Inside each pod was a motionless figure, suspended in a semi-foetal position. Frost covered the glass, and a thin layer of mist floated around the base of each pod. The next image was a close-up of a digital control panel. The screen displayed various graphs and data streams, with readings on cryogenic temperatures, heart rates, and brain activity.

Amidst the muttering from his coworkers, Bill described what he was seeing:

"I've got human-like bodies in liquid-filled pods, could be a genetics program."

"Human-like?" asked Jack. "Not just human? Or bodies?"

"Well, I wouldn't want to rule anything out… let's see what else we've got."

Without closing the open windows, Bill returned to the original folder and clicked on a file called "ALTERNATIVE 2". Inside this were photographs of sheer mountainsides with roads leading up to their bases and huge, heavily fortified, thirty-foot-high iron doors built into their sides. Further files showed schematic drawings detailing a huge silo, hundreds of floors deep below the ground, with housing, recreation areas, food and supply storage, and a massive armoury.

"OK, Alternative 2 has pictures of underground bunkers." Bill opened up a written document. "The heading is 'Deep Underground Military Bunkers'. D.U.M.B. Ha! Dumb."

"Nah, not that. That is good though, maybe I'll do a debunk on that… Go back to the untitled folder —is there anything about phlegm?"

Bill clicked and closed a few more folders, looking for a likely candidate.

"I've got FLEM, with an 'F', I guess that's it, right?"

He opened up a text document.

"Fault Line Expansion Mining, it stands for."

Bill scanned the document, which outlined a mining method of building Geothermal Power Stations, the main source of renewable energy used in the country. Bill's eyes widened as he read on.

"Christ, this is huge."

He clicked through files in rapid succession, leaving them open on the screen as he did so. Diagrams showing how the power stations needed to sit on fault lines in order to access the Earth's core heat sat alongside images of sinkholes. Bill could hardly contain his excitement.

"The explosions, they weren't terrorists. These people have been setting charges to deliberately create fault lines…"

"What? Why?" Jack was confused by this revelation.

"For Geothermal Power Stations by the looks of things. No wonder there've been so many earthquakes recently—this is unbelievable!"

"YES! This is it, Bill. This is massive. They're causing earthquakes and blaming terrorists. Oswald was right!"

"Who's Oswald?"

"Oh, I'll explain later. What else? Anything about Pandora? Or Phoenix?"

Bill located a file named Pandora and opened it up. His expression turned from excitement to concern as he turned to his assistant, who forgot she was supposed to be holding the phone for Jack to see.

"That doesn't look good," he whispered.

CCTV footage showed a chaotic scene, red emergency lights flashed rhythmically as scientists and technicians, clad in white lab coats and protective gear, darted frantically between workstations, their faces masks of terror. Heavy steel emergency doors descended rapidly, sealing off each section of the facility. The workers' fears turned to dread as the doors slammed and they realised they were trapped. Within seconds, a dark, viscous cloud began to seep into the room, rolling in like a malevolent fog. The cloud spread with an unnatural speed, enveloping the workers and the equipment in an inky shroud. They gasped and choked as the mist filled their lungs. Within moments, their skin turned ashen, and they collapsed to the floor, blood oozing from every orifice.

Jack could hear the gasps and alarm building in the room and demanded more information:

"What's happening? Bill, let me see!"

Bill ignored Jack's pleas and opened up a file labelled "PHOENIX PROTOCOL". Completely taken aback by what he saw, he turned to his assistant:

"Becky, is that what I think it is?"

6th November, 0915hrs

Jack was now out of his seat, pacing up and down the empty train carriage, staring at his phone, waiting to be filled in. The BBC centre was now coming up fast as he approached his destination. Remembering Jack, Bill took the phone back and looked right into the camera, his face a perfect picture of grave alarm.

"Jack, you won't believe this, are you sitting down?"

Jack was about to lose his mind with curiosity.

"Stop messing with me, man, just tell me what you found."

"OK, I'm just…"

In the distance behind Jack, a pale streak of light split the sky, following a perfectly perpendicular trajectory into the BBC Centre. With a deep BOOM! the train shuddered and the phone screen went black. Jack instinctively ducked and covered his head, unsure if the train track would survive another earthquake.

As the untroubled train pulled into the station, Jack picked up the phone and shouted into it.

"Hello? HELLO! Bill?"

Stepping out of the train and onto the platform, Jack saw a single plume of smoke rising from the old BBC building, which was circled by a huge cloud of dust, growing in size as it moved further from the epicentre. The building itself was virtually gone. On any other day, the world would have been up in arms, but today it went unnoticed. He dropped his phone and dropped to his knees, struggling to acknowledge what had just happened.

6th November, 0950hrs

Amidst the chaos, Oswald desperately searched for Sam, following the route of the tunnels above ground, looking for potential exit points. The earthquake had been little more than a tremor, but the general state of disrepair and makeshift nature of many homes had left the streets an almost unrecognisable mess of pallets and tarpaulin, sucked into cracks in the road or crushed by falling debris. If Sam was right about the earthquake they'd predicted, they were in for a horror show.

Oswald clutched his phone tightly, the screen displaying his most recent photograph of Sam, as he pushed his way through groups of people offering help or solace, occasionally stopping to show the screen with a desperate plea, "Have you seen her?" to anyone who would give him their attention.

As he navigated the broken streets, he witnessed the resilience of London's inhabitants. Despite all they had put up with over the years - the decline in living standards, the subjugation, the loss of rights - still they came together to help one another. Strangers became heroes, working together to retrieve possessions, provide care for the injured, or rebuild collapsed tents. Despite the devastation, the city's spirit had not been broken.

There was much chatter amongst the crowd about

the origin of the disaster. Oswald caught snippets of discussions as he rushed through the streets: some blamed the UnHeard, some said fracking, others called it a force of nature. To them, it was less important to know why than to deal with the consequences.

Stories of separated families reuniting spurred him on, but he was conscious of his upcoming deadline and the fact that if he did not find Sam soon, he would have to continue the mission without her. All he could do was hope that she had found her way out of the tunnel and was hiding until it was safe to connect, which was what he had trained her to do in such circumstances.

As he ran from manhole to dilapidated underground station, checking for signs of escape, his heart was heavy, full of regret for the life he'd provided her - one of secrecy to the exclusion of all the normal father-daughter activities. Had he been able to look the other way, ignore the moral corruption of his employers, they could have had a comfortable life in one of the better suburbs away from the city slums. A happy, if ignorant, life of cinema trips, sports clubs, and prom dresses, rather than training her to hide from CCTV cams, distrust the government, and lie to her mother.

Still, all that training had made her resourceful: if anybody could have made it out of that tunnel alive, it was Sam. Realising the time, he made the decision to regroup with Jack and get back to the plan. Sam knew they were heading for the BBC Centre, he just hoped she would be there when he arrived. He picked up the radio and called for Jack.

"Come in, Jack, over."

Jack was climbing over the remains of the BBC, turning over lumps of brick and concrete, panicking and breathless, in what he knew was a futile attempt to find his colleagues. He stopped to respond to Oswald:

"Don't come. Don't come here…"

"Why? What happened? Did they get the USB?"

"They… I think… I mean I know… they're dead. Everyone. I think there was a missile, it's completely flattened. Everyone was inside, Oswald, my whole team!"

Oswald's mind raced as he tried to make sense of the news, and a terrible realisation dawned on him.

"Oh God, the chip… they must have tracked it. DAMMIT!"

"You mean we led them there? I thought you were smart, how did you let that happen? You must have known!"

"The tunnels. We were supposed to take the chip out in the tunnels, they'd have lost the signal. The guy was too fat…"

Jack stopped and held the radio to his head, squeezing his eyes shut, pressing the ball of his hand against his temple and gripping his hair, as he did when he was stressed.

"What the fuck have you got me into here? People are getting killed, lots of people! This is insane! It's way out of my league, Oswald, I'm out!"

"It's too late for that, they're onto us, you're in whether you like it or not. Look, we need a place to regroup, have you got any ideas?"

Jack put the radio to his chest and looked around. He hesitated and grimaced before putting the radio back to his ear.

"Owen. I'm supposed to wake him up anyway. He's in the railway arch behind The Fox on Kingsland Road. I'll be there in twenty."

Jack let his legs give way, landing roughly in a seated position in a pile of rubble and held his head in his hands, covering his face to hide his tears as his shoulders shook uncontrollably.

Oswald was at his last stop along the route of the tunnels, a service exit stairwell. Looking down on the stairwell was a CCTV camera. Oswald pulled his coat hood further over his head and approached cautiously, as though slowing down the process would prevent bad news. It was clear that something had gone on: the door below was off its hinges, a sheet of OSB broken in half and sodden. Sitting in a pool of water at the bottom of the stairs lay a solitary trucker's cap, a string of LED lights hanging off its peak.

The White Room – Jack

"Yeah, that was hard. My workmates were like my family… apart from Nan, of course. It hit me like a sledgehammer." Jack shifted uncomfortably and sat on his hands as he spoke.

"How did that make you feel?" For the first time, the disembodied voice sounded concerned.

"Guilty. Scared. Mainly guilty, though."

"Why guilty? You neither started the sequence of events nor triggered the explosive."

"I don't know. I knew I was into something dangerous, but I was so wrapped up in the adventure. I could have kept them safe. I could just have used my Harker account to post the findings; there was no need to involve them at all. I brought them in so I could keep up my adventure. It's like, when I was a kid my dad would beat me, hard. Regularly. I'd have been put in care if my nan hadn't stepped in, bless her.

"The thing is, though, my mum knew it was happening—he beat her too, but she stayed with him, like she enjoyed the danger or something. I felt like she'd chosen this dangerous partner, but I hadn't, so I felt like it was her fault I was getting beaten. I think I blamed her more than him, even though he did the beating. This was the same; I'd chosen the danger, not them."

"About your mother, do you believe she enjoyed the relationship? Is it not more likely that she was afraid to leave?"

"I guess so, you don't think that way when you're a kid though. You just want someone to take you away, and that should be your mum. Anyway, I was my mum in this situation. Do you get what I mean?"

6th November, 1030hrs

Owen lived in his workshop, situated in an ancient arch beneath the looming shadow of a defunct railway, hidden from the bustling city. This secret haven was adopted by Owen as his base many years ago: he'd found it, patched it up, and fortified it against anyone who might try to take it from him. When renting a place of your own becomes impossible, you start taking, and Owen had scored well.

As Jack arrived, he found Owen up a ladder, reattaching electrical cables to an overloaded junction box.

"Oi oi!" called Owen as he spotted Jack, "Got a bit hairy this morning, didn't it? I thought my roof was coming in."

"You don't know the half, mate," came Jack's reply.

Owen climbed down from his ladder, taking in Jack's dishevelled appearance and red eyes. He wiped his hands on a rag and looked him up and down deliberately.

"Have you slept, mate? I was out like a light once I got in."

His thick Welsh accent had a way of dancing over words, with rises and falls that made things sound positive, regardless of the theme. Jack barely responded, instead leaning his back against the exterior wall and sliding slowly to the ground. Owen knew Jack well enough to recognise a serious issue.

"Come in, I'll make some coffee. You look like you need it."

Jack had never actually been inside Owen's place before. As he ventured deeper into the dimly lit space, he was greeted by a cacophony of disassembled gadgets, drone parts, camera components, and a labyrinth of metal shelves covered in small electrical engines. This ramshackle workshop was a sanctuary of chaos and ingenuity, not a million miles from Oswald's lair in content and appearance, although much bigger. The workshop bore the marks of countless hours of dedicated tinkering. Shelves lined with misshapen and mismatched containers held an array of widgets, circuit boards, and wires, sorted meticulously despite the apparent disarray. Drones with missing wings, cameras stripped of their lenses, and remote controls with buttons repurposed for other projects hung like peculiar works of art.

A makeshift workbench occupied the centre of the room, its surface cluttered with half-finished drones. Tools were scattered about, each bearing the scars of use, and wires dangled from above, forming a chaotic web that carried electricity to various contraptions in progress. Many of the gadgets had a thick layer of dust, presumably a result of the tremors rather than any lack of hygiene on Owen's part.

One corner of the workshop displayed a collection of furniture made from reclaimed wooden pallets and discarded materials. A coffee table fashioned from a warped pallet bore the weight of a stack of technical manuals and a cup of cold coffee. Nearby, a surprisingly comfortable salvaged chair had been adorned with a cushion made from an old flight jacket.

A curious juxtaposition against the cluttered backdrop was a bed tucked away in another corner. Sat next to a wardrobe and dressing table, the small square section of the space was immaculately clean and tidy, an oasis in amongst the clutter.

The end of the workshop was blocked off with an uneven wall of breeze blocks, with a heavy bookcase full of technical manuals, photography books, and classic novels, resting unsteadily against it.

The White Room – Jack

Jack had stopped telling his story and sat motionless, looking straight ahead, his eyes glazed over. The voice prompted him:

"Tell me about your relationship with Owen."

"Owen? What do you want to know?"

"What would you like to tell me?"

"Well, he was my cameraman. I'd do the reporting, he'd hold the camera."

"There was clearly more to your relationship than that. How did you meet?"

Jack stopped to think about that for a moment. It seemed like they'd always known each other...

"I was living up north for a little while, near the Welsh border. This was before the Bonfire Night attack; life was more or less alright back then. I didn't know many people, but there was a good pub where you could have some fun, you didn't really need friends to go there. He was one of the locals, you know.

"He hung around with a group of people I vaguely knew. We'd kind of nod hello, play pool occasionally, crack a joke or two. He was a laugh. That sort of knowing-him-without-knowing-him thing went on for a while. I didn't know his name, but I knew him to say hello.

"Anyway, one night I met this girl - she was very… enthusiastic, if you know what I mean. Pushy almost. Put it this way, if it had been the other way round I'd have been done for assault. So, you know, I went back to her place and all that… Her name was Ava Jones, and she reckoned I knew her brother, Owen.

"Now, the only Owen Jones I knew of was an absolute psychopath, mostly known for battering anyone he didn't think should be in the same pub as him. Particularly on Friday nights, as soon as the pub shut. Not someone you want in your life at all… Anyway, she was hot as hell, so I was trying to decide if she was worth the risk. Some blokes don't want anyone dating their sister.

"So, back at the pub the next day, I was with Owen and a couple of other pub randoms - bear in mind I didn't know his name at this point - and I asked them about Ava, did they know her? Was she Owen Jones's sister, and should I steer clear given the psycho she was related to?

"They all pissed themselves. Turned out there were two local lads called Owen Jones: one a psycho, the other was the Owen Jones I was talking to, and it was his sister. He seemed happy for me to be dating her though, so I arranged to meet her the next day.

"Now this pub had about ten concrete steps up to the door, and as I arrived, sme bloke came bouncing down those steps, head first. It was only about five o'clock, so no bouncers were on at that point to be throwing people out. I stepped out of the way so he didn't land on me, and who's at the top of the steps rubbing their fists better? Ava, proud as punch that she'd just knocked out her ex. Turns out she was a psychopath, never mind Owen. I stopped seeing her but carried on hanging around with Owen."

"How did you begin working together?"

"Just naturally. He was doing technical stuff; I was trying to be a journalist. At some point, we started needing help with things that the other one could do: I needed a bit of filming doing here, he needed a bit of help writing something there. It just kind of morphed into a permanent arrangement. After I got the Bonfire Night scoop, it was formalised because I had a proper job, with regular income, just as most people were finding themselves unemployed. I looked after him financially; he looked after me physically."

6th November, 1045hrs

Owen perched on the edge of his sofa, a Frankenstein's assembly of broken furniture parts, pallets, and blankets, his eyes wide in disbelief as Jack briefed him on the morning's events.

"Killed by a corporation? As in a business? Where people work?" he asked.

"Yeah, a really big but really secretive one."

"So no terrorists then. You must be disappointed…"

"Depends on how you define terrorists… anyway, I reckon this is bigger than The UnHeard."

Owen sat back for a moment, allowing the information to brew. His brow furrowed:

"And what are we supposed to do about this? Foil the baddies? We're not exactly Batman and Robin."

"I don't see this as a Batman thing; it's more like James Bond," quipped Jack, a cheeky grin spreading across his face. "Just as well really, cos you'd be Robin."

"Yeah right, like Robin could kick Batman's arse!"

"He was the brains, and the money, mate. I'm Batman."

"Fine, he's the worst hero anyway – a billionaire

living in a slum city who decides to spend his fortune punishing desperate people instead of helping them. You be Batman."

A loud banging at the door abruptly interrupted their conversation.

"That'll be Oswald," said Jack, jumping up to let him in.

Jack peered through a small gap in the poorly fitting door to see Oswald hovering close by, head down, hood up. Unbolting the locks, he dragged the door open, scraping an arced groove ever deeper into the rough concrete floor as it screeched.

Without thinking, Jack jumped on Oswald and gave him a long, tight hug, which Oswald loosely returned with just one arm, looking over Jack's shoulder to take in the wonders of Owen's workshop. Realising they might not be at the hugging stage just yet, Jack stepped back and straightened himself, ready to make the introductions.

"Owen, meet Oswald: he's the man that knows." Owen waved a hand in acknowledgement, and Oswald nodded. "Oswald, meet Owen. I look after him."

"That genuinely could not be further from the truth…" retorted Owen.

Formalities dispensed with, Oswald got on with

the job at hand:

"Did Jack fill you in?"

"The Illuminati are real and have killed everyone we know," Owen replied.

"More or less. Forget the Illuminati though, all those satanic ritual stories are red herrings. These are much worse. These are Capitalists."

"No word from Sam then?" asked Jack, genuinely concerned.

Oswald pulled Sam's sodden hat from his pocket and threw it onto the makeshift coffee table. He shook his head and dropped into an armchair, which groaned under his statuesque frame.

"That's not good," lamented Jack, picking up the cap to inspect. Oswald was more optimistic:

"Let's not jump to conclusions just yet. At least it looks like she escaped the tunnel. Hopefully she's gone to her mum's. Right now, we need to find out what Pandora is and how to stop it. If we don't, it looks like we're all dead."

"What, even me? Why do I have to die?" asked Owen, now more alarmed than he had been by Jack's tales.

"You, me, your friends, your family – everyone," Oswald explained.

"Hang on," interrupted Jack, "we haven't actually established that yet."

Oswald sat up and leaned in as he explained his theory.

"Not technically, no, but I know these people and there's more to this than meets the eye. What troubles me is that secrecy is everything to them, but they've become reckless. It's like it doesn't matter if they're exposed. They don't seem worried about providing explanations, it's desperate…"

"They have explained," Jack countered, "They said The UnHeard would attack the wall today."

"Has anyone seen a missile? Has the wall been hit? No. But there are big cracks in the roads and flooded tunnels. This isn't how they operate. There's no way they'd do something as huge and obvious as flood the underground without planning it and providing a solid story. They're not thinking ahead; they don't care if they lose credibility. I think what Sam heard was right. This is an existential threat."

Owen looked at Jack, not sure whether he believed the story. Seeing the doubt in Owen's eyes, Jack backed up Oswald's theory:

"Mate, if you'd seen what I've seen in the last few hours, you'd already be on board with this. I've got no reason to doubt anything Oswald says."

Owen turned back to Oswald and put his hands on his knees, as if ready to push himself up out of his chair.

"OK, so we're going to save the world today," he said, his Welsh lilt lending an air of hope.

"I'm going to save the world! I always knew I was special…" Jack jibed.

"Special needs maybe," Owen playfully retorted.

"That's no way to talk to your saviour."

Oswald frowned at the banter and decided he'd had enough.

"Listen. You haven't saved anything yet, and the odds are well against us. Doing this comes with serious risks; any of us could die in the process."

Owen took in Oswald's words, looking for some perspective. "What are the odds of us dying if we do nothing?"

"Well, that's the point, isn't it? If the information Sam found is real, and nothing we've seen so far suggests otherwise, we'll all die if we do nothing. I'm sure of that. I'm just not sure how it's going to happen. If we don't know how we'll die, we can't prevent it. The only way we can find out is to get inside Dynasty HQ…"

Oswald shrugged his shoulders and sat back.

"Well, how on Earth are we going to do that?" asked Jack. "We can't even get inside the walls now the tunnels are flooded."

"Good point," said Oswald. "And if we can't get inside the walls, we can't get on the roof."

Owen, who had been lost in thought for a moment or two, perked up at this.

"The roof of Dynasty? Why do you need to get up there?"

"There's a control box on the roof; it accesses the entire building's operations system. It's there in case of a fire, but it's impossible to access without permission. Even if we could get past the walls, we'd still need to scale the building, and then there's still the sentries at the top."

"Hang on," Jack patted his pockets as if he was trying to find something, "I might have some suction pads on me…"

Oswald glared at Jack, unimpressed by the quips. He was about to pull Jack up on his attitude when Owen piped up:

"I think I might have a way."

6th November, 1045hrs

When Sam eventually regained consciousness, she was alarmed to find herself unable to move. Thick nylon straps were buckled around her ankles, wrists, across her torso and forehead, pinning her down. She struggled against the straps for a moment, quickly realising it was futile.

Her restricted movement limited her view of her surroundings, but she could see a sterile glow emanating from recessed LED strips lining the ceiling, and vague pastel shapes, fuzzily reflected on the brushed aluminium walls. She could also tell that she was in the centre of the room, strapped to a gurney, with various cables and electrodes stuck to her wrists, chest, and neck. The room was long and narrow, with white cupboards built into the walls and a heavy armoured door at one end. Large ventilation grids in the ceiling fed air to the room, which, coupled with the lack of windows, suggested she was underground.

Hovering nearby was a mobile unit, equipped with a monitor displaying her heartbeat, plus some other numbers and readings she didn't understand. Below the screen, a selection of shiny tools: scalpels, pliers, a bone saw, shears, sat alongside some much more intricate-looking devices on which she decided not to dwell, all meticulously laid out and ready for use.

The room's atmosphere was suffused with an oppressive silence, broken only by the occasional drip or the faint hum of machines. There was a strong smell of disinfectant, leading Sam to wonder whether that was to prevent infections or cover up nefarious activities.

Sam's mind was racing: where was she? Who brought her here? What would they do to her? Were the tools just there to scare her?

With a hiss, a door slid open, and Lawson walked in, strip lights filling the room with a cold, much brighter light as he did so. Although she tried to hide it, Sam immediately recognised him and now understood where she was: this must be the bunker she had heard about when Lawson killed his subordinate. He approached, smiling.

"Good morning. My name's Lawson."

Sam remained silent, pursing her lips as she tried to squirm and twist her way out of the restraints.

"I assume you know why you're here. You've been very hard to find. I was beginning to worry we might not find you at all."

He paused and looked at Sam kindly, half-smiling as he spoke. "You must consider me a threat. It's a fair assessment; I am. To you. To your friends. Maybe your family…"

Sam's eyes darted from left to right, avoiding eye contact.

"I really am very impressed though," he continued, "You put yourself in exactly the right place at the right time. Or wrong place, depending on your point of view. How did you do that?"

Finally, Sam broke:

"I've no idea what you're talking about!"

"Oh, come now. You had no business being in our offices after midnight. Why were you there?"

"I just fell asleep; I left when I woke up."

"You really expect me to believe that?" Lawson's voice raised as he spoke.

"It's true!"

"I suppose the flash drive just fell into your bag as well?"

Sam shifted as much as she could under the straps.

"I don't know what you're talking about!"

Lawson leaned in, his face inches from Sam's, as he let rip.

"YOU KNOW EXACTLY WHAT I'M TALKING ABOUT!"

Sam tried to turn her head away, closing her eyes tight as she felt his hot, coffee-flavoured breath on her face, tiny flecks of spittle filling her ear.

"I swear I don't! I promise, I just left!"

Lawson stepped away and turned to the tray of

tools, picking each one up individually and inspecting them, as though looking for flaws. From the corner of her eye, Sam could see what he was doing, her voice cracking as she asked:

"Are you going to torture me?"

Lawson smiled wryly as he looked over his shoulder at her. Turning back to his workstation, he replied:

"Torture is fun, but it's never been particularly effective. People will say whatever you want just to stop the pain. You have to take them at their word, then go away and act on that information. Nine times out of ten it's not true; it's either what they think you want to hear or completely made up. I don't have time for that today."

Running his fingers over the tools, he settled on a TV remote and turned around to face Sam. Sensing her confusion, he pulled the workstation around so that Sam had a direct sight of the monitor and pressed a button on the remote. The screen switched to show CCTV footage from inside the conference room, footage which clearly showed Sam taking the flash drive and running away.

He paused the video, looked back at her, then back at the screen. Sam remained silent; clearly, there was little point in protesting further. He flicked the remote control again; this time, an aerial view of a suburban area came up, crosshairs hovering over the old BBC Television Centre.

"Do you know what you are looking at?"

Sam blinked slowly.

"And do you understand exactly where this view is coming from?"

Sam looked straight at him. Lawson raised his eyebrows, confident that she knew what he was talking about.

"This is the feed from Crossfire, my new favourite toy. It lives just outside our atmosphere, floating around until I tell it where to go. Right now, its missiles are locked onto your friends."

Sam took a sharp intake of breath, as if about to say something, but stopped herself.

"What, did you think we couldn't track our own microchips?"

"What are you going to do?" The panic was evident in her voice.

"That depends on you. How are you planning to stop the tenders?"

"Tenders? What's a tender? I don't know anything about tenders!"

"That's a shame. Let's watch."

He stepped out of the way of the video screen so Sam could see clearly.

"I don't know what you want me to tell you!" said Sam, breathlessly, exasperated that of all the reasons she should be there, she genuinely did not know what he was talking about. After a few seconds, a white flash filled the screen, followed by dust rising from the wreckage.

"NO!" screamed Sam.

"I wouldn't feel too bad, that was a recording. They died about 20 minutes ago."

Sam gasped, her mouth dropping open in disbelief.

"Shall we send it somewhere else?"

The White Room – Sam

"Describe how you felt during your captivity," said the voice.

Sam hesitated for a moment, her eyes glazing over as she reflected upon her ordeal.

"Scared, mainly. I mean, I definitely thought I was going to die there. I was pretty sure I'd just watched my dad get bombed, I'd definitely seen Lawson kill a man with his bare hands..."

"What stopped you from giving him the information he requested?" The voice was gently probing. Although it appeared at first to lack emotion, there was a distinct empathetic tone that put Sam at ease as she answered.

"For a start, I had literally no idea what he was on about. He'd got the thing about the flash drive right, but the rest was nonsense to me... tenders? He'd completely lost me."

"If you'd had the information he was asking for, would you have given it to him?"

Sam showed a flicker of vulnerability, knowing that ultimately she could not have saved anyone.

"That's a difficult one, all things considered..."

6th November, 1055hrs

Owen led Jack and Oswald to the back of his workshop and wrestled with the bookshelf that had appeared so precariously balanced against the uneven wall. It turned out to be on hinges, as Owen dragged the shelves round a large hole in the breeze blocks was revealed.

"Open sesame," said Owen as he pulled on a string with a flourish, to light up a secret room.

Jack and Oswald followed him through the gap, to find two large shapes covered by tarpaulin.

Owen grinned as he walked around the shapes and stood on the other side of the room, addressing his guests across the shapes.

"Are you ready for this?" he asked smugly.

"Just get on with it!" retorted Jack, unhappy with the idea of Owen keeping secrets from him.

With a magician's flair, Owen took a corner of the tarpaulin and dramatically hoisted it up and over his head.

"What do you think?" Owen grinned, waiting for approval.

Before them sat two machines, not dissimilar to motorbikes, but with horizontal rotors rather than wheels.

Jack circled the machines, in wonder. "Are they hover-bikes?"

"Yep," replied Owen, beaming.

Oswald walked over to inspect the machines, stroking the handlebars and crouching to assess the intricate mechanics. Jack could not contain his excitement.

"How long have you been hiding these? How did you even get them?"

"Built 'em. Last thing I did before they banned 3D printers."

Jack jumped on one and pretended to ride it, making aeroplane noises and ducking imaginary projectiles.

"This is definitely the coolest thing you've ever done. I don't see how it helps though; we can't just fly over the walls. But still though, HOVERBIKES!"

Oswald looked up from his inspection to back up Jack's point.

"He's right. Sentries will shoot down anything trying to cross the walls."

Owen responded with a teasing smile, "Not over, through."

"Oh right, did you 3D print a Ray-Gun while you were at it?" quipped Jack.

"Through the fans," Owen clarified.

Jack dismounted the bike, losing his footing slightly as he did so and hopping a few steps before regaining his balance and making his point.

"Through the fans? On these things?" He pointed up at the sky in disbelief as he spoke, "Is that even possible? Oswald, have a word..."

Oswald sized up the bikes and considered his rather daring proposition.

"You've tested these bikes, have you?"

"Yep, theoretically. I mean they fly, I've just not taken them out of the workshop. The tech is exactly the same as the drones, just bigger, with a car battery for power."

"How much weight will they take?" Oswald inspected the mechanics as he spoke.

"Two people, no worries."

Jack was incredulous: "Oswald, you're not seriously considering this, are you?"

Oswald raised his eyebrows, rubbed the back of his neck, and stood up to face Jack.

"Do you have a better idea?"

The White Room – Jack

"I didn't have a better idea," Jack admitted.

"How did you feel about risking your life?" asked the voice.

"Oh, you know, after we'd practised on the bikes, worked out a plan, got comfortable... I was shitting myself."

6th November, 1115hrs

By Dalston Junction, a set of six tower blocks stood close together. These had once been the height of luxury living for London's hipsters, a peculiar class who were wealthy but preferred to pretend they were not. Many of these hipsters had worked in the creative industries: graphic design; website development; photography; illustration. These were the first jobs to go with the advent of AI, despite the very same people believing that in an automated world it would be the creatives that would be kings. In attempting to stay ahead of AI, many of their specialisms had become increasingly niche, to the point of uselessness..

As it turned out, only those hipsters that had managed to secure a property portfolio, usually through an inheritance from family wealth they had denied, had survived the decline in the economy. Almost all of them had moved inside the walls for a life of leisure, with a few setting up countryside communes or leaving Britain altogether to enjoy their money in the sun.

As a result, the tower blocks now housed people lucky enough to work inside the walls, providing services for the landlords, and had fallen into a state of disrepair. Windows were broken, moss covered much of the exterior, and ivy cascaded from a series of communal patios, staggered at progressive heights between the buildings.

As they wheeled a trailer along Kingsland Road, avoiding the chaos, the cameras, and the cracks, Oswald outlined the advantages of starting their flights in this area.

"These blocks have very few cameras on them, you can see each one clearly from the ground."

He pointed out the cameras in question.

"They all point downwards, at the ground; they're not worried about anything happening higher up. We can weave from one patio to the next and keep out of sight as we go. Should be fairly straightforward."

He traced a path with his outstretched finger, zig-zagging between the buildings as he worked his way up from one patio to the next.

"That camera is turning one hundred and eighty degrees every sixty seconds, so as soon as it's perpendicular, we need to be on the bikes and heading for that patio on the sixth floor. Then we wait for the next camera and so on. Are we good?"

Jack and Owen nodded, although Jack's enthusiasm was lacking - heroics were not really his thing.

As Oswald watched the camera's movements, Owen snuck beneath the tarpaulin, tinkering with motors and getting ready to go. Jack shifted his weight from foot to foot, looking uneasily at the route ahead.

"Which one are we going to end up on?" he asked.

"That one, Labyrinth Tower." Oswald pointed at the tallest of the buildings, eighteen storeys high. "It's directly in line with a fan, nothing tall in between. It's perfect."

"OK, good. Probably makes sense for me to meet you up there, no?" Jack was never going to be controlling the bikes; he'd be Owen's passenger. "It will be quicker with one person on each, right?"

Owen nodded, "Yep. It's a lot of stairs though…"

"I'll get the lift!"

"Ha! Ok then," laughed Owen.

"OK, see you up there."

Jack jogged to the main doors of the flats, once a tall glass entranceway with a concierge, plants, and brightly coloured feature walls, now a mess of chicken wire and discarded bottles. Outside was an armoured vehicle of the type used by the Props, and a solitary guard stood at the main entrance, which stood ajar.

He dropped his head as he passed the Prop, who, to Jack's relief, paid him no attention.

Naturally, the lift was not working, leaving him to face the daunting challenge of an eighteen-storey climb. Standing at the bottom of his challenge, he looked up at the endless geometric spiral forming a continuous helical pattern that appeared to have no end.

He gripped the once-gleaming handrail and embarked on his ascent, taking care not to catch his hand on the sharp edges of the cracked and chipped metal. The steps themselves were no better: they had been built only for use in emergencies but were now worn and uneven, as they had replaced the lifts.

As he climbed, he navigated broken furniture, rotten food, and pools of urine. Flattened cardboard boxes surrounded by discarded food cartons, a sure sign that people were using the corridors as shelter, people who could not even gather the means to buy a tent, were evident on every floor.

Eight floors up, he met the Props again, grappling with an old couple who had failed to keep up with their rent. The old man, protesting the decision to evict, had his face pushed into the wall by the Props as they handcuffed him. His wife sat on the floor sobbing, powerless and scared as the Props fixed a metal grill to their front door.

"But we're only a month behind! Where will we go?" she pleaded.

It didn't matter to the landlords. Waiting lists for actual flats, in buildings made with bricks, were never-ending. Every time a new tenant moved in, the landlord could increase the rent, and for every tenant that couldn't keep up, there was a new one to take their place. If rent went up, they would just need to work more hours.

Jack considered stopping to interview the victims, amazed that on a day like today, with all the chaos in the streets, the Props were still focused on protecting the income of the landlords.

For once he managed to focus on the task at hand and took a deep breath: only ten more floors to go. He took to counting down the floors as he climbed, taking the stairs two at a time. He could make each landing in twelve steps, losing himself in the maths to take his mind off the strain. Twelve floors up, he was wheezing; by the time he burst through the final doors onto the top floor patio, he was red-faced, drenched in sweat, and clutching his chest as though in cardiac arrest.

Owen and Oswald were already there, discussing the practicalities of flying through a moving fan.

"Oi oi. You decided to join us then?" Owen chuckled.

Jack bent over, his hands on his slightly bent knees as he struggled to catch his breath. The sweat that had built up now served only to intensify the cold November wind, which burned his throat as he panted. "It's so cold up here!"

Owen provided no comfort. "You noticed. Wait until we're flying into the wind at this height…"

They regrouped by a tall glass barrier that enveloped the patio area, their vantage point overlooking north-east London, approximately fifty metres from the city walls. They were roughly level with the large, slowly rotating fan blades: a short flight, but the gun turrets across the top of the wall were an irresistible presence.

"OK, so it needs to be timed right, but the blades are moving slowly enough for us to get through, no problem." Owen was upbeat, but then he was used to the way these things handled, even if the drones he was used to were much smaller.

Jack, who was still getting his breath back, was less convinced.

"You're sure about this. What's to stop those guns shooting us out of the sky?"

Oswald chimed in on that question: "The guns on the wall point up; they're looking for anything trying to come over the walls. Sentries at ground level are only looking at the ground. This is our sweet spot, as long as we stay more than thirty feet off the ground and below the height of the walls, we'll be fine."

"And once we're on the other side?"

"Same deal. The gun turrets point outwards; they're not interested in anything flying away from the city. The next set of guns are on the roof of Dynasty HQ. You guys hover below roof level while I deal with them." Oswald mounted his hoverbike. "Are we ready?"

Owen climbed on his bike and nodded as Jack considered climbing on the back.

"I'm really not convinced about this…"

"Just get on and hold on tight. I promise not to go too high."

"We're already too high!"

Owen smirked. "It's cool, I've got this."

Jack was still reluctant:

"One more thing. So we land on the roof and then what? Abseil with fire hoses? You know that swinging-through-closed-windows thing doesn't really work, don't you?"

Once again, it was Oswald who provided reassurance.

"I have a plan. Wear these." He handed Jack and Owen small earpieces, like shiny white kidney beans. Owen put his in his ear, while Jack made a show of it, fiddling around as the earpiece repeatedly fell out. Owen and Oswald looked on with impatient frowns.

"What? My Nan says the only thing that should go in your ear is your elbow. Try it! It can't be done. Ergo, nothing should go in your ear."

Oswald decided to ignore Jack's faffing and carried on with his explanation:

"From the roof, we need to get down to the bunker. Well, you do; I'll direct you."

Owen flicked the switch to power up his bike as Jack climbed on behind him.

Jack had one more question for Oswald:

"What do we do when we get inside? Surely they'll see us?"

"That's where the control box on the roof comes in. I can tap in and control the CCTV, make sure they only see what I want them to see. You need to find a computer on the internal network and put this next to it."

He held a small plastic disc, with a flat button. Oswald pressed the button, and two tiny antennae protruded from its surface.

"It's a wireless drive – the only way to hack a closed loop. You get it inside, put it next to any computer, and press the button. I'll do the rest."

Jack looked at the disc with a blank expression as Oswald continued.

"It needs about 90 seconds uninterrupted, but once in, it'll take everything on their system and send it to me: CCTV, employee records, communications... everything. Ready?"

"Right now?" Jack still didn't feel quite ready for the flight.

"Unless you think we should stop for tea..."

Oswald's tone was undeniably sarcastic.

Jack inspected the wireless drive, one eye closed.

"And what's this thing again?"

Exasperated, Oswald turned to Owen. "Owen?"

"Don't worry, I've got this."

Jack reluctantly climbed onto the back of the bike and put his arms around Owen's waist. With a gentle turn of his wrist, they rose into the air and hovered for a few seconds.

"This isn't so bad," Jack declared, feeling a little more comfortable with the task.

Oswald shouted one last instruction before they set off:

"Don't hang around too long; we only need one Prop to look up and we're finished."

Owen twisted the throttle again, lifting them above the protection of the glass barrier and subjecting them to the force of the wind, which knocked them about as if riding a rodeo bull. Jack gripped Owen more tightly as they were buffeted by powerful, freezing gusts, and Owen struggled to set their course. Undeterred, Owen locked his sight on the huge, steadily turning blades and leaned into the wind, heading directly for the aperture. With metres to go, Owen accelerated and tilted the bike to the left, while Jack covered his eyes and screamed:

"NO NO NO NO NO NO NO NO!"

Owen, calm and composed, skilfully manoeuvred through the opening, narrowly avoiding the menacing blades. Once inside, the wind subsided and Owen hovered, once again in control.

Jack uncovered his eyes, relief flooding through him:

"YES!" he exclaimed, slapping Owen on the back as they waited for Oswald to follow.

"Jeez, you're a pussy sometimes," Owen teased.

"Excuse my healthy fear of death, mate, this isn't a computer game, you know. Besides, bravery is being scared and doing it anyway. On that metric, I'm braver than you."

Hovering silently, they watched the fan for any sign of Oswald.

"Oswald's taking his time, isn't he?" said Jack.

Owen manoeuvred the hoverbike from side to side, trying to get a better view, until Oswald's blurry figure could be made out between the passing blades, rapidly approaching.

Owen was worried: "He's not going to make it; he's not fast enough."

At the last moment, Oswald tilted the bike, just as Owen had, but he was too slow: just before he cleared the fan, the fan blade clipped the back of the bike, sending him spinning. He quickly lost altitude as he struggled to regain control, fighting to maintain sufficient height to avoid detection by the sentries below, while avoiding a collision with the side of Dynasty HQ. As he dropped, he fought with the handlebars, leaning against the spin to level out. Office workers inside the building remained oblivious, their backs to the window as he hurtled towards them.

Within a few feet of the window, Oswald composed himself, waited for the rotors to face the wall of the building, and gave the accelerator one last blast, pulling him out of the spin, restoring control, and rising quickly out of the workers' sight to hover alongside the boys. Owen's concern was palpable: "Steady on, mate; these things are not easy to come by."

Jack could not resist chipping in: "Yes, they are; you just print them!"

"Technically, yes, but I don't have a printer anymore; no one does."

"Guys, focus." Oswald nipped their banter in the bud. "The sentries on the roof have a blind spot. You stay here; I'm going to disable them. I'll call you when it's safe."

Oswald flew to the corner of the building and hovered below a sentry with a rotating camera. Watching for the camera to point away from him, he quickly rose to roof level and set down right behind it. As the camera rotated towards him, he dropped to the ground and pushed himself up close to the leg the sentry sat on, out of the camera's field of vision.

As the camera moved away again, Oswald jumped into action, expertly dismantling the gun's casing and pulling a single wire from its socket to disable both the camera and the gun, which dropped its nose like a guilty dog. Watching the next camera along, he waited for his moment and hurried into position, staying low behind air conditioning units to avoid the sentries on the other side of the roof. Again, once the camera pointed away, he disabled the gun turret before moving around and repeating the exercise on the remaining corners of the building to make the roof safe.

"OK, you can come now," he instructed, his finger to his ear.

While Owen and Jack pulled up and landed, Oswald had located the control box, pulled off the lid, and was busily connecting wires to a screen. As the screen flickered to life, Jack and Owen approached.

"You took your time, didn't you? What if we were spotted?" asked Jack.

"I thought you'd probably prefer it if the guns were disabled first," he replied.

As Oswald typed code into his tablet, the boys watched over his shoulder, much too close:

"A little space, please?"

They took a step back as Oswald swiped through files, expertly navigating his way through a rapid succession of screens and security measures until he located the elevator controls.

Immediately, an exterior lift rocketed upwards, stopping a couple of metres below roof level.

Owen went to the edge of the building and looked down on the immaculately kept, beautifully modern cityscape below. Jack joined him in surveying the deserted city, surprised that only armed Props and the occasional city worker could be seen.

"Where is everybody?" asked Owen.

"I guess they're keeping out of the way of the made-up terrorists."

"You're fine with that, are you? You'd normally be calling Oswald a nut and trying to debunk him."

"Yeah, well. I've learned a few things this morning, made me question everything I've ever reported on…"

"What, you mean apart from the UnHeard stuff?"

"Yeah. Here's one: you know how they banned 3D printers?"

"Yep."

"You know why, right?"

"Guns. People were using them to print guns; there was that school shooting."

"That's what I thought, but it's not what Oswald reckons. He says they were banned because they were killing corporate profits. No one was buying anything; they were just printing what they needed from open-source code."

Owen looked doubtful: "Doesn't explain the school shootings, mate."

"It does if they were staged to make it look that way, for an excuse to ban them. I'd have called bullshit on that if I hadn't seen... all this. They don't actually do the killings; it's all about data. They use it to identify people who can be manipulated into extreme actions, then press their buttons. A fake news story on their Harker feed, an unfair job dismissal, then eventually a link to print a gun. Get enough of those in the works, and you've created a puppet who'll do your evil bidding, and no one can touch you for it."

Jack's voice cracked as he struggled to finish his sentence, thinking of his friends from work and the terrible end he had led them to. He looked out across the city rather than speak, embarrassed by his show of emotion.

Oswald, who had finished his fiddling, stood up and spoke impatiently. "Boys! Are you with us?"

Jack rolled his eyes at Owen before turning back to Oswald. "All yours, mate."

Oswald joined them at the edge of the building and pointed to the top of the exterior lift shaft, where a series of cables hung from a huge pulley and motor, suspending an elevator. "That's where you guys are going."

Jack looked the lift up and down, slightly confused: "How do we get in? I don't see a hatch."

"You don't get in; you get on," replied Oswald.

"On? We're twenty storeys up; I'm not sitting on top of that thing! And it's halfway down the building."

Owen had moved to the top of the shaft and was studying the drop: "It looks OK to me. I reckon it's safer than the hover-bikes…"

"You said they were safe!" Jack exclaimed.

"They got us here, didn't they?"

Oswald interjected at this point: "Even if you could get inside the elevator, it wouldn't work. There are cameras inside; anyone could stop the lift and get in… plus, security in the bunker is tough; you wouldn't get past the first door."

Jack looked over the edge of the building and shuddered.

"Stay on top of the elevator," Oswald continued. "You'll avoid detection that way. When it stops at the bottom, you'll find a removable access panel on the wall of the shaft. Go through that, and you can follow the air vents to any room in the bunker."

"Sounds a bit corny. Hey, what's that really old movie where the guy crawls through air vents and beats the terrorists?"

"Die Hard?" suggested Owen.

"That's it. Die Hard. We're going to die. Hard."

Oswald, ignoring Jack's protestations, decided to direct instructions towards Owen.

"Owen, I need you to watch his back while he sets this up. Don't forget, the drive needs 90 seconds; it can't be interrupted."

"No worries, we've got this," said Owen, reassuringly, before taking the gadget, positioning himself on the edge of the wall, and dropping down to the roof of the lift below.

Jack looked gingerly over the edge of the building:

"It's a very long way down…"

"Rubbish; it's six feet. Just lower yourself down. I'll catch you."

"I mean to the ground!"

Inhaling deeply, Jack perched on the edge of the wall, his extended legs outward. With a deliberate twist, he doubled over, quickly shifting his grip on the wall, his abdomen now bearing his weight. With the grace of a newborn giraffe, he lowered himself down, his feet scratching frantically at the wall, before dropping the last six inches to join Owen.

With Oswald controlling the lift from the roof, they began their descent on the outside of the building. Jack and Owen sprawled flat on the roof as it dipped below street level and entered a vertical tunnel, passing within a few feet of an oblivious Prop. The shaft enveloped them in darkness, pierced only by the ever-diminishing circle of light coming through the hole above them. The journey was swift yet smooth, culminating in a sudden, controlled halt.

Using the torch on his phone, Owen located a circular handle set into a metal panel on the wall, a couple of feet above the roof of the lift.

"This must be it."

Jack looked on as Owen tried to turn the handle.

"It's not opening. Which way is open, clockwise or anticlockwise?"

"Righty tighty, lefty loosey," replied Jack, twisting each hand in turn.

"You're such a child… anti-clockwise then."

The handle still wouldn't turn. Owen put his hand to his ear as he tried the hatch again and spoke to Oswald.

"OK, we've got it, but it seems to be locked. Or

extremely stiff..."

There was a brief pause as Oswald typed instructions and swiped his screen. A faint but discernible "clunk" came from inside the hatch.

"Try again; it should open now."

Owen tried the hatch again. With a jolt, it yielded.

"OK, we're in."

Oswald breathed a sigh of relief, pleased his plan was working.

"I'm not going to lie; I was not one hundred percent sure that was going to work. Get inside; I'll direct you."

Owen crawled into the aluminium tube and moved into the building, quickly followed by Jack.

"Right, you need to keep going for about fifteen metres, then there should be a hatch on the left. Wait there until I say so."

Oswald flicked through more screens, each one bringing up a camera for a different area, until something caught his eye, causing him to reevaluate.

"Slight change of plan. Jack, give the drive to Owen. I've got a new job for you."

6th November, 1145hrs

Lawson pulled the tool table closer to Sam, positioning it directly in her eyeline. The screen now showed an aerial view of a suburban street beyond the slums, far enough from central London to be unaffected by the devastation the morning had seen so far. This was where the middle classes lived, people with white-collar jobs who mostly worked from their rented, but reasonable homes. In the centre of the screen was an end terrace house with crosshairs ominously hovering over it.

Lawson broke the silence, "I take it you recognise the view?"

Sam hesitated; this unfamiliar perspective momentarily confounded her. Yet, as her eyes scanned the scene, the communal basketball court, the neighbour's broken trampoline... she realised with a jolt: this was her home. More importantly, it was her mother's home, and she would be there.

"What are you going to do?" she asked, her voice sharp with urgency.

"That largely depends on you..." Lawson replied coolly.

"But my mum's there; she has nothing to do with this!"

"But you do, don't you? Just tell me what I want to

know."

Sam struggled in vain against her restraints. She tried again, screaming with the effort, but the restraints were strong and allowed for virtually no movement. She glared at Lawson, frustration filling her eyes, as she recovered from the effort. Anger, an emotion she rarely gave in to, was surfacing.

"How do I know it's not a recording?" she grasped at this slim hope. "You could have blown her up already!"

Lawson's smirk betrayed a sinister amusement. He seemed to be enjoying the prospect of her fear turning to fury, particularly as she was so helpless.

"Ah, I have another toy; you'll like this."

He took the remote control and pointed it at the screen. The display flickered and split into four, each offering a disconcerting glimpse into the interior of the house. The angles were odd, not places you would choose to set up cameras if you were planning it.

In the bottom right-hand window, Valerie could be seen at the kitchen sink, washing dishes, oblivious to the imminent threat.

"Check the time on the clock," Lawson instructed, pointing to the clock on the screen and then gesturing to the clock on the wall of the bunker. Both read 11:40. Sam tried her strength against the restraints once more.

"How are you doing that? When did you put cameras in?"

"It's good, isn't it? It's called Jackdaw. It allows me to take control of any camera on any device within range of my drone, which is currently sitting in your back garden. So..." he tilted his head in mock empathy, "do we have an understanding?"

Sam started to cry, unsure what else she could do:

"Please, don't hurt my mum, she's done nothing! I don't know what you want from me!"

Lawson spoke forcefully:

"I want to know who you are working for and how you plan to sabotage the evacuation!"

"Evacuation? From what?"

Lawson was incredulous at Sam's apparent ignorance:

"From Pandora! When the virus escapes, we're all done, everyone. Finished. If I have to kill your mother to avoid that, I will consider it a small price."

Sam stopped crying for a moment as the weight of what Lawson had just said sank in.

"Pandora's a virus?"

For the first time, a look of doubt flashed across

Lawson's face. Could this have been a coincidence? Shaking that concern off, he continued to press Sam for the information he needed:

"Last chance, tell me the truth or I'll order the strike."

Sam took another look at her mother on the screen, blissfully unaware of the danger she was in. Realising she had to do something, she broke down in tears:

"OK... I do work for a temp agency, I am just a cleaner! I fell asleep and when I woke up I heard you talking about FLEM, and then about Pandora escaping and killing people! Then you killed that man, and if you'd kill him you'd kill me, so I just ran!"

"Now we're getting somewhere. Why did you take the drive?"

"I don't know. It seemed like the right thing to do. To let people know."

"Which people? How did you intend to warn people?"

"Jack Klein, he's a reporter. He'd have been in the building you bombed."

"Did you give anyone else a copy of the drive?"

Crying, Sam nodded her head as much as she could against the restraints.

"I made a copy, that one's underwater in the tunnels. Was that you too?"

"An old flood defence system. And the other?"

"You know about that one, it went in the drone to White City."

"Excellent."

A high-pitched beep interrupted Lawson, distracting him from the task at hand. He stepped away from Sam and lifted his wrist to talk into his watch:

"What is it?"

"Sir, the comms system seems to have developed a glitch. It's probably nothing; we're still dealing with a few problems following the quake, but I thought you should know."

"I'm coming now."

Lawson took a roll of gaffer tape from a drawer in the workstation and tore off a six-inch piece.

"I think you have more to tell me." He leaned over Sam and covered her mouth with the tape as he spoke. "I'd use this time to gather your thoughts. Don't go anywhere."

He turned his back on Sam and walked towards the door, smiling at his joke. He waved his hand and the door opened with a quiet hiss, revealing a Prop, who Lawson addressed as he passed him:

"Nobody comes in or out of this room apart from me, is that clear?"

The Prop nodded and Lawson walked on, then paused to reiterate.

"Nobody!"

6th November, 1145 hrs

Navigating through the frigid labyrinth of aluminium tunnels was a bone-chilling venture. Jack and Owen pulled their sleeves over their hands to counter the cold and muffle the metallic groans their movements caused if they did not proceed with extreme care. They slid along on all fours, their way lit by occasional vents, until they arrived at a junction.

"Left or right?" whispered Jack, hoping Oswald could hear him.

"This is where you split up. Owen, you go left. You'll see a hatch about five metres in. Once the room is clear, you can climb down. You'll have about two minutes before you need to get out again. It's 11:49 now; we need this whole thing done in less than ten minutes. Are we clear?"

Owen repeated the instruction to confirm his understanding, "Five metres in, gadget on, two minutes, out."

"OK, good. Jack, you go right, then first left. Wait at the next hatch for my instructions."

"Gotcha."

Upon reaching the vent, Owen peered down into the small room, illuminated by the glow of computers and the solitary figure of the unsuspecting operator. In hushed tones, he reported back to Oswald:

"OK, I'm here."

Oswald's voice came through Owen's earpiece in a crackling whisper:

"I'm looping the camera feed now. I just need to get the operator out. Unless you can deal with him?"

Owen, crouching above the scene, assessed the situation. The computer operator was a scrawny figure with oversized headphones, immersed in the soft glow of computer screens and lost in the digital realm. As the operator adjusted his glasses and emitted a subtle sniff, Owen grinned:

"I think I can handle him."

With the meticulous precision of a covert operative, Owen gently lifted the hatch, sliding it silently to the side. He removed his shirt and wrapped the fabric around one hand, taking care not to knock the aluminium walls as he did so. Preparing for the descent, he lowered himself through the hatch, landing silently behind the unsuspecting operator.

Immediately, Owen flicked the shirt open and wrapped it around the operator's face, muffling any potential outcry. With practiced efficiency, he used the shirtsleeves like reins, pulling the man backward and twisting as they fell, landing with

Owen on top, his knees on the nerd's back.

Securing the situation, Owen deftly bound the operator's wrists with the shirt's sleeves, creating an improvised hogtie that left the man incapacitated on the cold bunker floor. With the operator immobilized and helpless, Owen located the wireless drive and whispered to Oswald, "OK, we're good to go."

As Owen pressed the button on the device, initiating the transfer, he leaned in close to the subdued nerd, "I'm sorry about this, mate. It won't take long."

Meanwhile, Jack approached the hatch he was looking for:

"I'm here. How do I open this thing?"

"It's open, you just lift it. Don't go yet though, wait for my mark."

Jack lifted the lid and lowered his head through the hole to survey the room below.

Still strapped to the bed, Sam spotted the back of Jack's head as he poked it through the hatch. She tried to call him, but the tape muffled her voice.

"MMMNNRRRGGG!!"

Jack twisted his head awkwardly to see Sam.

"SAM! You're alive! Any idea how I'm supposed to get down from here?"

"MMMMUUUUNNNMMM"

"Yeah, I thought you might say that."

Jack clumsily lowered his legs through the vent, his legs flailing below him, looking for a non-existent platform until the momentum of his swinging legs pulled him through the hole and crashing to the ground.

"That wasn't as cool as I wanted it to be," he opined.

He winced as he pulled himself to his feet, then rushed over to Sam, hugging the whole bed before starting to unbuckle the restraints.

"I knew you weren't dead! This is amazing! I know we've only just met, but I feel like we're connected now, you know?"

The words spilled out of him as though the chaos of the day had forged an unbreakable bond. He stopped unbuckling the straps and sat on the stool, turning away from her, his head bowed in a rare display of vulnerability as he confided in her.

"I know I seem like a confident, popular guy, but the truth is my only real friends were at work. They just got killed right in front of me…"

Sam's eyes widened in urgency, silently pleading for his attention as she struggled against her bonds, but he continued regardless.

"Aside from Nan, I've only got you, Owen, and

Oswald left. I feel like we're properly bonding, especially now I'm rescuing you. What do you think?"

He briefly turned to face Sam, who was staring at him in desperation, mouth still taped, shaking her restraints.

"Oh shit, I'm supposed to be rescuing you, aren't I? My bad."

Jack peeled the tape from Sam's lips, allowing her to respond for the first time:

"For God's sake, can we do small talk later? I'd really like to get free."

"Fair enough," said Jack, as he resumed the task of releasing Sam. "Ha! I'm actually rescuing you right now! I'm a proper real-life hero, saving the damsel in distress. This will definitely be going in my memoirs…"

Sam grimaced at the thought.

"You know what this means, don't you?" Jack stopped unbuckling and looked at Sam, a self-satisfied grin etched across his face. "I'm the hero…?"

He raised his eyebrows and waited for her to click, which she deliberately did not.

"You're the girl…" he prompted.

Sam was not impressed by his take on the situation and took the opportunity to cut him down to size:

"Oh my God, do you know what? I think I might stay here. Oh, and for the record, you do not come across as popular and confident, you come across as a dick."

"Bit harsh, you're not free yet," he shrugged, before suddenly realising: "I should tell Oswald!"

Jack continued unbuckling the straps with one hand and touched his earpiece with the other.

"Oswald! Guess who I found! It's Sam, she's alive. I'm rescuing her now!"

Oswald was unimpressed, "Are you always this quick on the uptake?"

"OK, she's free. What next, boss?"

Oswald had been dealing with the data transfer as Jack fell through the hatch and was annoyed that he had not followed instructions.

"I told you to wait, now I need to sort a diversion or you'll be caught."

Noticing the way Jack touched his ear as he spoke, Sam grabbed his head and talked into the earpiece.

"Dad, there's a deadly virus about to be released, and Lawson's threatening to kill Mum!"

Without the earpiece, she was unable to hear Oswald's answer.

"Not how they work!" complained Jack, pulling his head away sharply, before repeating Oswald's reply. "He says to stay calm, he's going to get us out of here. Did you say virus?"

Back in the data storage room, Owen was still sitting on the operator's back with his shirt off, nervously counting the seconds. With fifteen seconds to go before the transfer was complete, the door opened with a tell-tale "hiss" and Owen found himself in Lawson's imposing presence.

Owen looked up sheepishly, fully aware of the trouble he was in.

"This isn't what it looks like..." he said with a smile, before launching himself at Lawson and catching the towering figure off guard, disrupting his balance and forcing him to the ground. Seeing Lawson on the floor, Owen tried to jump over him and make a run for it. Lawson's reflexes were sharp; he caught Owen's foot and with a masterful twist brought him crashing to the ground.

Both men sprang to their feet, a charged tension hanging between them as they locked eyes, each calculating the other's next move. Owen, driven by desperation, struck first—a futile attempt to shift the odds in his favour; a quick jab followed by a forceful haymaker. He was no match for Lawson, who slapped Owen's fist upwards, raising it just enough to allow room for a sharp prod into his armpit. He followed up immediately with rapid, surgical blows to pressure points on Owen's torso, leaving him disabled and unable to defend against a final, devastating chop to the throat. Unimpressed by his attacker, Lawson nonchalantly adjusted his tie and left Owen for dead, requesting a clean-up through the intercom as he left the room.

As he left, lights started flashing red, and a blaring alarm filled the air. Over the tannoy, a robotic voice declared:

"*INTRUDER ALERT! ALL GUARDIANS TO SECTION FIVE! INTRUDER ALERT!*"

Without hesitation, Lawson sprinted toward section five, acutely aware that this was where Sam was being held captive, rallying additional Props along the way.

In the interrogation room, the flashing lights spurred Jack and Sam to make their escape. Looking around the room, Jack was unsure of the best plan and turned to Oswald for help.

"Oswald, how do we get out of here?"

"The way you came in, obviously," came the reply, much to Jack's dismay; falling down through a hatch was much easier than climbing up through one. Jack eyed the hatch, realising it was beyond his reach, and scratched his head nervously.

"Erm..." he mumbled, searching for a solution. The bed was too heavy to move, leaving the torture table the only option to make the height they needed. He wheeled it to the hatch and gestured for Sam to join him.

"Come on, I'll help." Jack offered, interlocking his fingers to provide a step up.

Sam put her foot in his hands and raised her other foot onto the workstation, but as she shifted her weight, they both forgot that the station was on wheels. The workstation traveled away from them, forcing Sam into the splits before the table toppled over with a loud crash as the torture tools hit the floor.

Jack struggled to contain his giggles as he apologized. He extended a hand to help Sam to her feet, but it was too late! The door slid open, and the Prop stepped in.

"OI! STOP THERE!" the Prop barked, reaching for his gun.

Without thinking, Jack charged toward the guard, head first. The Prop easily sidestepped Jack's attack, the butt of his gun thudding against the back of his neck as he passed, slamming him into the aluminium wall, which buckled under the force.

Shaky and disoriented, Jack peeled himself off the wall and turned to face the Prop, his fists raised in a feeble attempt at combat readiness, his mind racing through his options: fight (this seemed unrealistic); run (where to, he couldn't outrun bullets); joke (if only his mind was working properly).

He remained motionless as the Prop advanced toward him, gun raised and ready to shoot. The Prop lifted his wrist to report his find, but before he spoke came a heavy THUD!

The Prop crumbled to his knees, revealing Sam standing behind him, staring down at the blood-stained shears now embedded in the Prop's back.

Wide-eyed, Jack stared at the guard, then back at Sam in disbelief. Sam, shoulders hunched and mouth agape, silently picked up a towel from the floor and wiped the blood from her hands. She took a deep breath, which she exhaled slowly through tightly pursed lips as she composed herself.

"We should go," she said, her voice steady as a rock.

Sam returned to the task of accessing the air vents, while Jack remained motionless, still processing what had just happened.

The White Room – Sam

"Had you ever killed before?" asked the voice.

Sam was indignant. "No, of course not!"

"How did it make you feel?"

"I don't know. I don't think I felt bad about it; just, sort of, nothing. Is that strange? It's strange, isn't it? I always thought killing somebody would be the sort of thing to haunt you forever, but nothing. Nothing at all. It was just the necessary thing…"

Sm stared into the distance, her palms pressed together and tucked tight between her thighs.

The voice reminded her of their earlier exchange:

"You said previously, that you lacked emotions when your father died."

"I did say that…" Sam stopped to think about that for a moment. "Oh my God, am I a psychopath? Or is it sociopath? Which one doesn't feel emotions? It's psychopath, isn't it? I don't want to be a psychopath, I'm just normal."

Sam was very upset by this notion. She'd always considered herself to be a good person, with a healthy respect for others. Certainly nothing resembling a psychopath.

The voice pressed a little further:

"Does your reaction to death concern you?"

"Yes!" she exclaimed, emphatically. "I thought I was normal, but that's not normal, is it?"

"Do you believe there is something wrong with you, for reacting this way?"

"I don't know. I've never had to think about it too much… apart from with my dad. There was a guidance counsellor at school when he died, but by the time I spoke to her, I'd already found out he was alive, so I had to fake it. I'd always told myself that I had some sort of connection to him, that I instinctively knew he was still alive, so that's why I wasn't mourning. Does that make sense?"

The voice did not reply.

"Also, maybe I blocked it out as a defence mechanism, you know? I read about that once: by not allowing yourself to feel anything, you avoid psychological damage, limit the trauma, especially for young people. I remember feeling like I related to that when I read it. Yes, defence mechanism, that sounds more like it."

Satisfied for now, she couldn't help being disconcerted by the direction the questioning was taking.

6th November, 1155 hrs

From his vantage point at the control box on the roof, Oswald flicked through the CCTV cameras he now commanded, surveying the movements of the Props to aid Sam's escape. As a former senior employee, he knew the building well and used this to his advantage. Spotting Lawson marshalling his forces and heading back to the interrogation room, he called on Jack:

"Are you out yet?"

"Nearly—it's not as easy getting up as it was getting down," replied Jack, as Sam pulled him up into the shaft.

"I'd get a move on; you've got company," Oswald warned.

"Yeah, I'm hanging around 'cos I like the atmosphere." He couldn't resist sarcasm, despite the urgency.

"I'll buy you some time."

Oswald kept Lawson and his men on screen, waiting for them to enter the corridor leading to the holding room. The corridor was long, with a series of strategically placed sliding doors, installed for security and defense purposes. Oswald bided his time as Lawson led his men through the first door, waiting for the last man to pass through. Just as the last man came through the first door and it hissed closed behind him, Oswald disabled all doors on that floor.

Lawson, expecting seamless access, swiped his wrist across a panel to open the door, but to his surprise, nothing happened. He tried again. Still nothing. A flicker of confusion danced across his face before transforming into rage. Turning to the camera, he started shouting, fury bursting from his eyes. Not that Oswald could hear anything; he smiled gently as he watched Lawson punching dents into the aluminium door, rattling the camera as he did so, as if anger was the key to the door. Content that his opponent was held for now, he returned his attention to Jack and Sam:

"Where are you up to?"

"We're out, sitting on the lift now," replied Jack.

"Good, I'll bring you up."

The lift lurched slightly, causing Sam to grab Jack's arm as it began its ascent. As the lift accelerated, Lawson's men prised open the door and rushed to the interrogation room, only to find Sam gone and the Prop face down in a pool of blood.

Lawson took a moment to think, taking in the scene: the dead Prop, the open vent, the door controls. This was coordinated by someone with inside knowledge of the company. There was only one place they could be going.

Oswald was still navigating through the files Owen had sent as the lift reached the roof and Sam's head appeared over the wall. Using Jack's head and the lift's cables as a ladder, she was already halfway up onto the roof.

"Dad!" she cried.

Oswald looked up and grinned, rushing over to throw his arms around Sam and pull her the rest of the way off the lift.

"I thought I'd lost you."

"You'll have to try harder than that," she joked. "Listen, what about Mum? Lawson was threatening to kill her."

"Don't worry, without you in captivity it would be pointless, he won't waste his time."

"But we're still getting her though… right?" Sam nodded her head as she spoke, as if providing Oswald with the correct answer.

"One thing at a time. Let's figure out what's happening first."

"But he said he had less than an hour. We need to get her!" She grabbed Oswald by the wrist as she spoke, her voice raised. Oswald shook his hand loose as he replied:

"We will. I'm just saying we need to know what we're dealing with before we work out what to do next. We should have everything we need on here." He tapped his laptop, the transfer now complete.

"DAD! You're avoiding her! Even now!"

"I'm not avoiding her."

"You are! All this time, you said it was too risky to tell her you were alive. I can't believe you! I'm calling her."

Sam snatched a phone from Oswald's bag of tricks.

Oswald grabbed the phone from Sam. "Don't do that!" His tone becoming notably sterner.

Sam was having none of it:

"Oh my God! Just last night we were talking about you. She still loves you, y'know, and look at you, ready to just abandon her while the world probably ends."

Oswald sighed and looked down at the phone.

"She doesn't love me, Sam. Maybe she loves the idea of me, the rose-tinted memory of me, but not me. Even if she did, we need to be realistic; I might not get through this alive. You really want to put your mum through my death twice? Let's just get off here and think about it when we're safe."

In the light of her time with Lawson, Sam could not see the sense in this.

"You're scared to face her. You're nothing but a coward!"

From the edge of the roof, Jack's voice called out in search of help.

"Don't worry about me, guys. I'm fine."

Sam defiantly turned her back on Oswald and went to help pull Jack up onto the roof.

Clambering over the side, Jack looked around for his partner. "Where's Owen?"

Oswald was packing up his kit and responded without looking up:

"He didn't make it."

Jack looked at Sam and back at Oswald, as a nervous smile spread across his face:

"What do you mean, didn't make it?"

As he zipped up his bag and threw it over his shoulder, Oswald looked up at Jack.

"I mean he ran into Lawson." His voice was devoid of emotion. "We need to go, right now."

Jack refused to accept what Oswald was implying:

"We're not leaving Owen!"

"We're not waiting. He's either dead or captured. We have to go!" snapped Oswald, irritated that he was having to play the bad guy to the youngsters.

For the first time, Jack displayed a temper:

"Use your thing! If you can find Sam, you can find Owen!"

Ignoring his outburst, Oswald walked toward the bikes. Jack jumped in his way, furious at being ignored, and pushed him back as tears welled in his eyes. Oswald stared at Jack for a moment, not sure whether to be offended or impressed, then pulled the tablet from his bag and plugged the cable into the control box.

"OK, one more scan then we go. I suppose we owe him that much." He handed Sam his laptop, touching the scratchpad to open a file. "Here, watch this. I'll look for Owen."

Jack and Sam looked at the screen which showed the Sad Clown speech made on behalf of The UnHeard, which had been broadcast on the walls earlier that day.

"I've seen this already," said Jack.

"I'm sure you have. Thing is, it was filmed and saved on these servers last night. That video was made by Dynasty," Oswald added.

Happy that Oswald was looking for Owen, Jack was instantly distracted by this:

"What, so Dynasty are The UnHeard? This story keeps getting better; it's gonna be huge!"

"Better?" asked Sam, once again taking issue with his phrasing.

"Oh yeah, deadly virus…" acknowledged Jack. "Exactly how worried should we be by that? Do I need to call my Nan?"

"Lawson said that if he doesn't stop it, the human race is over," said Sam.

"OK? So quite worried then… eight out of ten, do you think?"

"He said that Pandora's an unstoppable virus." She faced Jack but spoke so that Oswald heard. "And HE won't let me call Mum."

Jack looked over Sam's shoulder to address Oswald directly:

"Oswald, did you hear that? What are we going to do?"

Oswald, having found no sign of Owen, was packing up again:

"Well first off, we get out of here, then we figure out a plan. I have the info I need now, but we're running out of time." He turned to Sam. "Lawson said he was trying to stop it?"

"He didn't say he was trying to stop it exactly… the main thing was he thought we were trying to sabotage tenders or something. I mean, what on Earth is a tender?"

"Well, he's either talking about chicken or small boats." For the first time, there was a hint of alarm in Oswald's voice. "Neither makes much sense at this point. Either way, we need to get out of here now."

"Not without Owen!" cried Jack.

Sam joined him in blocking the way to the bikes, her arms crossed defiantly:

"I'm not moving until you give me the phone."

Oswald weighed up his options. He could easily push Jack out of the way and get to the bikes, but what about Sam? There was no time for phone calls.

As Oswald decided on his next move, the door onto the roof burst open with a BANG, and a cleaner dressed in a full hazmat suit barged past them toward the bikes, yelling as he ran:

"MOVE… NOW!"

Confused by this, the trio stood and watched as the cleaner mounted a hoverbike.

"QUICKLY!" he shouted, pulling back his hood. Jack was overjoyed as Owen revealed himself, rushing over to give him a hug. Shrugging off the hug, Owen was insistent that they needed to move:

"I really mean it, Props are coming, we have to go!"

Grabbing the crowbar from his bag, Oswald rushed to the door and slid the metal bar through the handle to secure it. He turned back to Jack and Sam as the door started rattling.

"The door won't hold for long. Go now. Sam, go with Owen; I'll hold them off."

"No, I'm staying with you! I don't know who this guy is!" she pointed out, not having met him before.

Oswald put his huge arms around her and effortlessly lifted her up onto the back of Owen's bike, despite her struggling. As she continued her protest, the bike lifted off the ground unevenly, causing her to grab hold of Owen.

"He's a good guy," Oswald assured her.

Owen calmly took control of the bike and flew off the side of the building.

"I'll be right behind you!" yelled Oswald as they set off.

With that, the door burst open and a Prop appeared with a line of Props behind him, waiting to make it through the door. Oswald kicked the first Prop heavily in the chest, pushing him back through the door and blocking the path of the others. Oswald wrestled with them, taking advantage of the bottleneck the door provided, grabbing rifle nozzles to prevent them aiming in his direction and putting all his strength into pushing the narrow door closed.

With no intention of joining the fight, Jack mounted the second bike and started the engine, calling to Oswald as he did so:

"Oswald! Come on."

Oswald, his back to the door, knew there was no way he could make it to the bike without releasing the Props and putting Sam in even more danger.

"JUST GO!" he shouted at Jack.

Jack hesitated, looking back and forth between Oswald's fight and his escaping friends, ultimately deciding he would be of little use to Oswald – there was no point in them both dying on that roof.

Jack kept looking back over his shoulder as he flew away, shadowed by an undeniable pang of conscience: could he really abandon Oswald? He struggled with the guilt as he flew from the scene before the sound of a machine gun brought him to his senses. He couldn't leave Oswald to die.

He manoeuvred the bike, executing a tight turn that brought him circling back to the building and ascending behind the defunct sentry. With the melee at the door distracting the Props, he landed silently and unnoticed, the faint whir of the hoverbike masked by the noise of the huge, noisy air conditioning unit and the raucous at the door.

By now, the Props had forced the door open and pummelled Oswald mercilessly with the butts of their guns, brutally forcing him into submission. At the edge of the roof, another chilling threat emerged, as a Prop unpacked a rocket launcher and proceeded to take aim at Owen and Sam.

Jack, crouching behind the sentry, looked desperately for anything that could save either party. The Prop with the rocket launcher was almost ready to fire as Oswald's captors forced him to his knees, obscuring him from Jack's line of sight.

As he shifted his position, he noticed the wire that Oswald pulled out of the sentry to disable it. The Prop now had Oswald flat on the floor, face down, putting him out of the sentry's line of sight: would reattaching the wire re-arm the sentry?

Jack fiddled with the wire, his hands shaking as he tried to force the splayed wires back into the tiny hole they'd come from; the more he pushed, the more frayed they got. Inspecting the hole more closely, he found a tiny screw blocking the wire. The Prop at the roof's edge now had the rocket launcher on his shoulder. He hastily turned the screw with his fingertips to make room for the wire as a Prop pointed a pistol at Oswald's head.

Jack licked his fingers, twisted the wires into a point, took a deep breath, and tried again. Just as the Prop was about to pull the trigger, the wire slipped into position.

BRATATAT! BRATATAT! BRATATAT!

The sentry's weapon sprang into life, rapidly targeting and shooting all the Props with pinpoint precision. In just a couple of seconds, all the Props around Oswald were dead.

The Prop with the missile launcher turned around, more slowly than he might without the cumbersome weapon on his shoulder. Jack ripped the wire back out of the sentry and sprinted at the Prop, landing a heavy shoulder barge in his chest. The weight of the missile launcher caused the Prop to topple backwards over the barrier, falling to his death many floors below as the missile shot off harmlessly into the air.

"Whoah-ho-ho. Nice work!" cheered Oswald as he sat up, for the first time properly impressed by Jack. "I didn't think you had it in you!"

"Now we can go," replied Jack, settling into the role of hero as he climbed back on the hoverbike and started the engine. Oswald grinned, got to his feet and ran towards Jack and the hoverbike. As he mounted the bike he paused for a moment:

"Thanks for coming back, Jack. You didn't have to do that."

Jack shrugged and looked at the ground, but before he could reply, the door to the roof crashed open again. Without thinking, Jack ducked down behind the bike.

BANG! The report of a gun split the air, and Oswald's expression changed from a purposeful grimace to a sad, resigned smile. He slumped over the hoverbike and coughed, causing specks of blood to spatter from his mouth. He tried to lift himself up and start the bike, but he was coughing more, his breath rasping and gurgling as the blood spilled into his lungs and he struggled to clear them.

BANG! A second shot caused Oswald's body to contort, as if electrocuted, before falling over the bike to the ground, his body and huge trench coat completely covering Jack.

Lawson strode across the roof to check Oswald was dead, unaware that Jack was hidden beneath his colossal frame.

"You always were an idealistic fool," he whispered, as he pressed Oswald's throat to check for a pulse.

Content that his opponent was dispatched, he walked to the edge of the roof, taking a rifle from a Prop as he did so. In the distance, he spied Sam and Owen making their escape. Raising the gun, he adjusted the sights, rested the mount on the wall, and calmed his breathing. With the lightest of touches, he squeezed the trigger to let off a single shot.

As Owen guided the bike towards the walls, the sound of gunshots was alarming Sam, who kept looking back over her shoulder for Oswald and Jack.

"They're not following! We need to go back!" she shouted.

Unable to turn his head to see, Owen pulled the

bike around in a circle to return to Dynasty. As he did so, Lawson's shot found its target, hitting the nose of the bike and sending it spiralling toward the ground.

They hit the ground hard, nose first, ploughing a deep furrow into a perfectly manicured flowerbed. An ornamental rock halted the bike with a jolt, throwing them over the handlebars to land face down, sprawled across a small patch of grass.

Back on the roof, Jack remained hidden under Oswald's limp, heavy body. He moved an arm slightly, surprised by the weight, to see Lawson at the edge of the building, handing the rifle back to one of the Props.

He could hear instructions being doled out: although he was unable to make out the specific words, it was clear that they would be leaving at any minute. He just needed to stay still and quiet until then.

Warm blood was still leaking from Oswald's chest, running over the back of Jack's neck and gathering in a pool around his face. Jack was struggling to stay still, trying not to gag as Oswald's warm blood ran across his face and touched his lips.

As the last Prop exited the roof, Jack stayed frozen for as long as he could, resisting the urge to retch, desperate to get the blood off his skin.

Finally, after thirty seconds that felt like thirty

minutes, Jack was convinced there were no more Props to worry about and set about getting up. He struggled to lift Oswald's considerable weight, instead wriggling, pushing limbs and the folds of his huge overcoat aside, until eventually he was able to roll the lifeless corpse to the side and haul himself out from underneath.

Exhausted from the effort, he wiped the blood from his face, lay back, and took a moment to stare at the smog-filled sky.

The White Room – Jack

"What made you go back for Oswald?" asked the voice.

Jack shifted in his seat, as if being uncomfortable in this magical chair was possible.

"I don't know, maybe I liked feeling like a hero for once."

"So it was to serve your own ego?"

Jack looked offended:

"No, that's not fair. If I was serving anything it was duty—I mean, how would I have faced Sam if I'd just left him there without trying to help?"

"So it was fear of how leaving him would make you look?"

"NO! Partly maybe. I did want to save Oswald—you have to remember how many friends I'd just lost. I suppose I was trying to make up for that in some way."

"If Sam had died in the floods and it was you, Owen, and Oswald trying to get off the roof, do you think you'd have gone back for Oswald?"

Jack sat and pondered that question. He knew the answer; he just wasn't prepared to admit it.

6th November, 1215 hrs

Owen and Sam picked themselves up and brushed off the soil. They were in the centre of the vast open square adjacent to Spitalfields Market, completely exposed. Staying low, Owen inspected the bullet hole in the nose of the hoverbike.

"What now?" Sam queried, her eyes reflecting the uncertainty that loomed. Owen cast a glance back at Dynasty.

"It doesn't look like they're going to let us go," he gestured toward a fleet of approaching armoured cars in the distance.

A series of bullets knocked out an irregular beat in the ground behind them. They ducked behind the bike, but it provided little protection.

"We can't stay here; eventually one of those bullets is going to get us," said Owen.

Used to protecting Jack, he seized Sam's hand, steering her towards the refuge of a nearby multi-story car park.

"What are you doing? I can run by myself, thanks," insisted Sam, trying to pull her hand free.

"We can hide in there," Owen asserted, keeping hold of her hand and running toward the entrance. As they darted across the square, Props gaining ground, the cacophony of bullets ricocheting off buildings and parked cars underscored the urgency of their flight.

Sentries suddenly stood proud like meerkats, each turn of their heads deliberate, rapid, and precise. They found their target, letting out a flurry of bullets as Sam and Owen entered the relative safety of the car park.

Once inside, Owen dragged Sam upward, the labyrinthine barriers offering limited concealment from the pursuing Props.

"Why are we going up?" asked Sam, doubting his tactics.

"Because there isn't a down," Owen replied, his focus on the immediate escape route.

"But we're trapped when we get to the top!"

"Let's worry about that when we get there. Right now, I'm more concerned about being away from the bullets."

"That makes no sense! Why am I following you anyway? Who even are you?" Sam demanded, frustrated.

"I'm Owen. Didn't Jack say? Look, we can hide up there and double back while they're looking. It'll be fine," Owen reassured her, with the air of a man who was entirely used to being in situations such as this.

As they ascended toward the roof, the distant

sounds of Props traversing the car park reached their ears. Radios crackled with instructions, a chilling reminder of the imminent danger.

"Team one, take level one: cover all exits. Team two, level two..." a disembodied radio voice instructed. It was hard to tell if he was really right on top of them or if the brutal concrete walls were playing games with echoes. "We need them alive if possible."

"If possible!" Sam whispered in disbelief.

For the second time that day, Sam found herself relying on the cold, damp walls of the disused car park for protection. As they shuffled through the levels, every sound they made seemed to be amplified by the empty, echoing walls.

As more Props entered the building, Sam and Owen stopped worrying about the noise they were making: van loads of Props were arriving, with no such concern about staying quiet. Hundreds of footsteps now bounced around the building, radios crackling with fuzzy instructions, far too loud. Had the Props stayed silent, they could have tracked the pair from the sound of their hearts beating against their ribs.

With the noise from the Props disguising their movements, Owen and Sam were able to move quickly. Props were covering all exits and taking positions on the ramps, forcing them to continue their ascent toward the roof.

"OK, maybe this wasn't the best plan…" Owen conceded as he sneaked a look back through the barriers. "We've got to keep going."

"We'll be trapped!" Sam half-whispered, half-screamed.

"Well, what else are we going to do? We'll figure something out, maybe there's a fire escape or something."

"There's not," said Sam, staying crouched and reluctantly following Owen up the last ramp to the roof.

As Sam had predicted, the open-air roof offered no refuge. There were no hiding places, no vehicles, no fire escape, no alternative way down. There was no furniture, bins, signposts… nothing that would provide shelter of any sort. Just four waist-height walls, a ramp leading up to the roof and a ramp leading down, both of which were filled with Props, leaving them exposed and with nowhere left to turn.

A troop of Props filed out into the open square and took position in a perfect line, their guns raised and trained on Sam and Owen, who dutifully raised their hands in surrender.

Lawson followed the Props onto the roof and stood to face his captives. He looked at his watch, paced back and forth a couple of times as if deciding on his words. Taking position at the end of the line of Props, he checked his watch one more time before addressing them:

"I'm going to give you one last chance. How do you intend to stop the tenders?"

"There's nothing I can tell you!" screamed Sam in desperation, "I don't even know what a tender is!"

Lawson frowned and with pursed lips, let a short, sharp sigh out through his nostrils:

"Very well." He turned his back on them and addressed the Props. "Take aim."

Sam and Owen looked at each other in panic, could this really be it? The Props stepped forward in perfect unison, drawing level with Lawson as they did so. Dropping to one knee, they steadied their aim as they waited for the instruction to fire.

With a CRASH, a hoverbike suddenly rammed into the line of Props, knocking them all to the ground like skittles, guns scattering as they fell. As the hoverbike tipped, Jack was thrown off, his landing softened by a layer of sprawled-out Props.

The hoverbike careered over the Props and straight for Lawson, forcing him to dive out of the way and land flat on the floor, his suit ripped and his face badly grazed on the tarmac. Momentarily stunned, Lawson lifted himself off the ground and paused on all fours as he struggled to compose himself.

Without hesitating, Sam rushed straight at him, sweeping up one of the Prop's guns from the floor and in one fluid motion, she gripped the gun by the barrel and swung it like a baseball bat, smashing into Lawson's temple and dropping him again. Owen kicked the remaining guns away from the Props, keeping one gun to prevent them from coming to their boss's aid.

With Lawson down, but not out, Sam gave him no room for manoeuvre, her small stature suddenly irrelevant as she stood over him, raining down repeated blows to his body and head. It was all Lawson could do to curl up and cover his head as the beating continued and Sam unleashed her rage, prefacing each blow with an exclamation:

"Threaten my mum?" WHACK! "You don't threaten my mum!" WHACK! "You don't mess with me!" WHACK! "You don't mess with my family!" WHACK! "And I don't know anything about your FUCKING PODS!" WHACK! WHACK! WHACK!

Sensing that Sam was prepared to keep going indefinitely, Jack came up behind her and reached out to take her by the shoulders, intending to pull her back so that they could make their escape before the Props recovered.

As Jack's hands made contact, Sam spun round to face him, pointing the gun at Jack's face as he lurched away from her, the butt to her shoulder and her finger on the trigger, ready to fire. Jack recoiled, his hands up by his shoulders:

"Whoah, steady!"

For a moment, Sam looked as though she might go through with it, being so lost in rage that she failed to register who she was pointing the gun at. She was breathing heavily, almost hyperventilating. Tears and snot ran down her face but she calmed down enough to realise it was Jack, until she noticed his blood-soaked clothes:

"Why are you covered in blood?"

Jack looked down to the ground.

"Jack, whose blood is it?" she continued, "Where's Dad?"

He looked back up at Sam, shaking his head.

"I tried, honestly. I even got a bunch of them."

"NO!"

Sam returned to beating Lawson, using the gun like an axe, blood starting to spatter across the floor as Lawson's ability to protect himself failed. Jack and Owen watched on with a mixture of respect and fear, aware that they could not stay where they were for long.

"How long do you think we should let her go at it?" Jack asked Owen.

"I'm not sure we get much say in the matter to be honest."

As they tried to decide on a course of action, the sound of more Props approaching made their minds up. Jack caught Sam's arm mid-swing:

"Sam! We need to go."

"HE KILLED MY DAD!"

"I know. We still need to go or they'll kill us too." For once, Jack found the appropriate tone; "Don't let him die for nothing."

As Jack dragged her to the hoverbike by the elbow, she tried to keep hitting Lawson, thrashing out with her feet when she could no longer use the gun. Owen gathered up the guns and threw them over the car park wall, then took his place at the front of the bike.

With three people aboard, the hoverbike struggled to take off, rising, falling, and tilting as Owen squeezed the throttle in bursts, creating just enough thrust to clear the car park walls.

Realising that the bike did not have the power to get them away from the advancing Props, Owen spoke to the group.

"It can't take all of us. I think the knock from the fan has damaged the battery too. We'll have to land and go on foot."

"Go where?" asked Sam, aware that they were no closer to a solution to the unfolding situation.

"Somewhere without gunmen, ideally," interjected Jack.

As the hoverbike lost altitude, Owen steered it toward a clear section of the street, fifty metres from the car park, leading to an open square. They landed roughly, but in one piece, and with gunfire bouncing off the road around them, made a dash for a shop doorway.

They huddled together; the doorway kept their bodies out of the line of sight of the oncoming Props, but offered no actual protection: they needed to move.

"What now?" asked Jack, turning to Owen for guidance, "We're not going to be safe here for long."

On the far side of the square, a section of the city walls could be seen, catching Owen's attention:

"Look over there, at the walls."

In the distance, the city walls had fundamentally changed; the smooth interior wall had folded downwards to reveal a series of small pods sitting on platforms the length of the walls. It was hard to see details, but they looked similar to miniature submarines, only with more glass and clearly pointing skywards. Limousines and helicopters were arriving nearby and small groups of people were being ushered onto the walkways between them.

"What's happening?" asked Jack.

"Tenders," said Sam.

Jack looked confused.

"That's what he meant by tenders. A small ship used to transport passengers to a bigger ship," she explained.

"I'm not sure you're being as helpful as you think you are," he retorted. "Ships need water. The river's on the other side of the wall."

With a crash, the window of the shop shattered, and any sense of safety they had felt shattered with it. Without thinking, all three ran into the street, covering their heads with their hands as if they provided some sort of protection against the bullets.

As they passed, a sentry jerked into life, its camera suddenly alert to their presence. It took a second or two for the gun to activate, giving them time to duck behind a large stone sculpture before the rapid fire of bullets pummeled the statue.

Pinned down by the gunshots, the trio were stuck.

"Are they still coming after us?" asked Jack.

"Nah, it's sentries," replied Owen, "That makes it harder."

"Shit, that's me," said Sam, "I'm the only one they can target."

"I reckon they'll know who all of us are by now. Speaking of which, you should have seen me back on the roof of Dynasty. I took out six baddies!"

Owen was impressed:

"Shit son, look who's becoming a man!"

"And I pushed a guy off the roof. He was aiming a rocket launcher at you."

"Nice!" said Owen with a grin. They took a moment for a high five, which was met with a hail of bullets as the tips of their fingers peeped above the shelter of the sculpture.

Sam grabbed their arms and pulled them down impatiently, out of the line of fire:

"Do you mind? I've just lost my dad, you know."

"Sorry," said Jack, "I'm not used to being a hero…"

"Whatever," she continued, "Look, we need to move. If sentries are locked onto us, they might have drones locking onto us too. Lawson's got some mad gadgets."

"I really don't fancy moving much," Jack raised his head slightly as he spoke. Immediately, bullets smashed into the sculpture and the shop behind them.

"FUCK!" he screamed, covering his head and dropping to the ground.

"Listen, we're dead if we stay here and that's definite," pointed out Sam, "If they don't get us, Pandora will."

"Listen, how certain are we of this?" Despite everything he'd seen that day, Jack was not completely convinced, "I've seen no actual proof, just your word."

"You're just too scared to move," she pointed out.

"We're being shot at. Scared is the reasonable response."

Once again, Owen interjected;

"Can we deal with the current, unbelievable, situation for now?"

"I say we go for the main gate," suggested Sam.

"That's where the Props are!" pointed out Jack.

"The walls," said Owen, "We need to get to the walls."

As they quarrelled, a Prop emerged from a side street, flanking their position. He hurriedly hoisted a rocket launcher to his shoulder, the sculpture in his sights. As he took aim, Owen looked up from the group and spotted him. He grabbed Jack by the hood and barged his shoulder into Sam, rugby-tackling her to the ground and forcing all three of them away from the statue and the oncoming rocket.

BOOM! The sculpture behind them exploded, spraying lumps of marble and concrete with the shockwave. A huge cloud of dust rose, temporarily hiding them from sight as they got to their feet and regained their senses. Owen ushered them onwards, blindly stumbling their way through the chaotic mess.

As the dust slowly settled, a new group of Props came into sight, putting pursuers on three sides. The sound of bullets bouncing off walls surrounded them as they ran, desperately looking for cover as the street opened up into a square. The best they could do was run, with no particular plan other than to keep moving.

As Owen led the way towards the walls, he faltered, as though he'd suddenly remembered something. He stopped running and paused for a moment, his arms outstretched as though trying to balance. Running straight past him, it took Jack a moment to notice Owen's strange behavior, but he slowed and hopped to a stop, confused but with enough faith in his friend to follow his lead.

"What's up?" he called.

Owen just held a finger up as if he was waiting for something. Then he crouched slightly and put a hand to the ground.

Jack became aware of a deep rumbling sound, which was accompanied by a slight vibration below his feet. The sound grew louder as the vibration became a shake. Everyone had now stopped moving, waiting to see what was about to happen.

As the shaking intensified, subtle tremors escalated into a violent upheaval that seemed to defy the laws of nature. The sound grew from a distant rumble to an all-encompassing roar, drowning out any attempt at communication, reaching its crescendo with a deafening BOOM.

The ground beneath their feet seemed to be trying to throw them off like a rodeo bull, lifting and tilting as though some monstrous force were attempting to break free from its earthly confines. A colossal crack split the square in two, sending shockwaves rippling through the air and throwing anyone in its vicinity to the ground with a force that left them breathless.

Meanwhile, the storefronts lining the square succumbed to the earthquake's fury, their windows exploding outward in a shower of glass shards that rained down upon the streets below. Lintels dropped from doorways like guillotines, their descent accompanied by the ominous sound of cracking masonry as walls buckled under the seismic strain.

Amidst the chaos, alarms blared their warnings, adding to the cacophony of destruction that enveloped the square. And then, as if to add insult to injury, a lone sentry post, standing sentinel on the outskirts of the square, lost its mooring and crashed to the ground, its mounted weapon spraying bullets into the air like a deadly hailstorm.

Finally, after what felt like an eternity but lasted only a few seconds, the shaking subsided, leaving behind a scene of utter devastation. Owen was the first to act, scrambling to his feet and crouching low, his eyes scanning the chaos around them. The earthquake had stirred up a thick cloud of dust, blanketing the square in a veil of obscuring cover that provided a momentary respite from their pursuers.

Racing over to where Jack lay pressed against an ancient drinking water fountain, Owen reached out a hand to help his friend to his feet. Jack, his head covered by his arms, looked up with wide eyes, his face a mask of shock and disbelief. But there was no time for hesitation.

"Come on, quick!" said Owen, "They'll be coming."

Jack looked up from his protective ball and poked his head out from the fountain, but was unable to make out the Props through the mess. Instead, he found Sam.

"We should go. Now!"

Emerging from the protective shroud of dust and debris, Sam's urgent words spurred the trio into action. With hearts pounding and adrenaline coursing through their veins, they knew their only option was to reach the pods before it was too late. As the dust settled, revealing the chaos around them, their eyes were drawn to the walls where the tenders awaited their desperate passengers.

Approximately three meters from the ground, the

new walkway beckoned like a lifeline dangling just out of reach. The tenders, raised from the walkway by massive clamps protruding from within the walls, stood out amidst the destruction with their sleek design and futuristic appearance. The vehicles' undersides were adorned with cones, such as you might see on a rocket, while their smooth white exteriors gleamed in the dim light of the devastated cityscape.

Gull-wing doors, clear and pristine, were raised for access, inviting the fleeing populace to seek refuge within their confines. Their overall shape resembled a soft triangle, with additional fins at each apex, giving them an aerodynamic elegance that belied their function as vessels of escape. Spaced evenly along the walls, the tenders stood like sentinels, offering hope to those desperate enough to brave the perilous journey to reach them.

But as Sam, Jack, and Owen raced towards the walls, they were acutely aware of the danger that lurked around them. Limousines, their occupants undoubtedly seeking refuge within the safety of the tenders, fought their way through the damaged roads in a desperate bid to reach the walls. Helicopters hovered overhead, their searchlights cutting through the dust-filled air as they sought stable ground amidst the chaos below.

Meanwhile, the walkways were a hive of frenzied activity as people hurriedly made their way to the waiting tenders, their faces etched with fear and desperation. The sickening sound of bullets ricocheting off nearby statues constantly reminding them that they were not alone in their race to safety. The Props, determined to prevent their escape, unleashed a barrage of gunfire in their direction, their weapons flashing in the dim light like vengeful spirits.

To make matters worse, the ground beneath their feet trembled with increasing frequency, each tremor growing stronger and more intense than the last. With every boom reverberating through the air, the cracks in the ground spread like the branches of a tree, making the terrain even harder to navigate, threatening to send them tumbling into the abyss below with each step.

As Owen effortlessly navigated the obstacles, leaping from bench to post box to lamp post with the agility of a seasoned acrobat, Jack and Sam found themselves on the opposite side of the widening crevice, the ground crumbling away beneath their feet with alarming speed. They ran with all their might, their hearts pounding in their chests as the sound of gunfire echoed through the air.

With each step, the crack in the ground widened, threatening to swallow them whole. Bullets whizzed past them, tearing through the air, leaving destruction in their wake as they took chunks out of statues and water features around them. The

Props, relentless in their pursuit, seemed oblivious to the chaos unfolding around them, their sole focus fixed on the fleeing trio.

"Why are they still shooting at us?" Jack shouted above the din of gunfire, his voice tinged with incredulity. "Have they not noticed the world's ending?"

Owen, perched atop the walkway, pointed to a sentry hanging loosely from the wall, its mounted weapon spraying bullets in all directions as it swung wildly from side to side. The recoil of each shot caused it to thrash about uncontrollably, creating a deadly hail of gunfire that threatened to cut them down where they stood.

"It's a sentry!" Owen's voice carried over the chaos, "Look, it's come off its hinges. Get behind something!"

With bullets whizzing past them and the ground crumbling beneath their feet, Jack scanned the area for cover, his eyes landing on a police truck parked next to the wall, one wheel sunk in the ever-widening crack caused by the earthquake. Without hesitation, he motioned for Sam to follow as they sprinted towards the relative safety of the vehicle.

Reaching the truck, Jack and Sam dove behind it, their breaths coming in ragged gasps as they sheltered from the storm of bullets raining down upon them. The ground continued to tremble beneath their feet, each tremor threatening to add a new branch to the crevice and pull them into the abyss.

After taking a moment to catch their breath, they clambered up the side of the police truck, between the truck and the wall to avoid the bullets. The truck was about five feet from the wall, with the walkway about three feet higher than its roof. It was an awkward, but not impossible jump. Jack sized it up for a moment, then made a desperate leap, coming up slightly short and leaving himself dangling precariously from the bottom of the railings. He swung from side to side, kicking his left leg up towards the walkway. Owen caught Jack's foot and managed to haul him up, just as another burst of gunfire echoed through the air, bullets ricocheting off the metal walkway with deafening pings.

Meanwhile, Sam, determined not to be left behind, assessed the distance to the walkway with a calculating gaze. With a glance at her petite frame, she was filled with doubt.

"It's too far, I won't make it - I'm too small!" she called out, her voice tinged with hopelessness.

"If Jack can do it, anyone can!" Owen retorted. Even now, he could not resist teasing Jack.

Determined to prove her worth, she eyed the battered truck for an alternative route, her mind racing as she sought a solution amidst the chaos. As the gunfire subsided momentarily, her eyes landed on a battering ram attached to the side of the truck; a six-foot-long, heavy metal pole with six handles staggered along the side. Thinking quickly, she freed it from the truck's side, its weight proving to be a formidable challenge as she struggled to hoist it onto the roof.

Balancing the battering ram upright, she took a deep breath, her eyes scanning the chaos surrounding her before she pushed the ram towards the wall. With nimble agility, she scaled the pole as it fell towards the wall, using its handles as makeshift steps. As she reached the top, the battering ram crashed into the walkway. Jack and Owen caught her arms and pulled her over the rails, panting as she collapsed onto the walkway, relief flooding through her veins.

Owen led the way to the empty tender, but as they neared their goal, another rumble shook the ground, causing the damaged walkway to collapse beneath Owen's feet. With a cry of alarm, he tumbled to the ground below, landing awkwardly on his left wrist.

With bullets still flying, Jack leapt from the wall to help him, pulling him behind an abandoned limousine for cover. As Owen cradled his injured arm, they both looked up at the broken walkway, neither finding a clear route back up.

"Come on, I'll push you up." Jack interlocked his fingers to provide a step for Owen.

"No mate, leave me – you'll never make it back up on your own!"

"Can we just for once give the 'Jack's-a-wimp' thing a rest? I'm in hero mode!"

"Go on then, give us a hand." Owen conceded.

Owen climbed up onto Jack's hands, then shoulders, then finally stood on his head to get up onto the wall. Sam reached down to help him up, and they both leaned perilously over the edge of the walkway in the hope they could help Jack, who scrambled desperately to find another route to safety.

Jack jogged along the base of the wall until his eyes fell upon a sturdy tree standing firm by the wall, its branches reaching out like beckoning fingers. With a surge of optimism, he began to climb, ignoring the scrapes and scuffs from the rough bark as he shuffled his way towards the walkway. He hadn't climbed a tree in years; it was harder than he remembered.

With inches to go, a deafening BOOM! reverberated through the air, and the ground beneath the tree gave way with a sickening crack. In an instant, Jack was swallowed by the gaping maw of a new sinkhole, the earth swallowing him whole as the tree vanished from sight. The ground trembled with the force of the collapse, and part of the wall buckled under the strain, sending another section of the walkway cascading downwards to form a makeshift ramp to the ground below, an empty tender left teetering on the edge of the precipice. With a faint glimmer of hope in his eyes, Owen turned to Sam:

"I might be able to get him."

Sam's eyes widened with disbelief. "With what?"

But before she could protest further, the sharp crack of gunfire echoed through the air, forcing them to duck behind the nearest tender for cover. Owen, undeterred, crawled out onto the unstable walkway, his injured arm forgotten in the heat of the moment. But Sam, her voice filled with fear and desperation, reached out to pull him back.

"How can you help with your arm like that?"

Owen's resolve was unwavering. "I can't leave him," he declared, his voice filled with determination as he kicked free from Sam's grasp and pressed on towards the edge of the walkway.

As they squabbled, a hand appeared over the top of the sinkhole: Jack was pulling himself up by the root of the tree.

"JACK!" called out Sam.

"I'd never realised how long a tree's roots are!" exclaimed Jack as he climbed.

Owen scurried down the fallen walkway to take Jack's hand with his working arm. As he pulled Jack to the walkway he nodded at the tender still sitting there, empty.

"We need to get in there."

Jack was unsure: "We don't even know what it is!"

"Yeah we do, it's a tender."

Jack turned to Sam for support. Instead, she glared at Jack and very deliberately followed Owen to the tender.

As Owen cautiously approached the sleek, futuristic escape pod, he couldn't help but be impressed by its design. The exterior gleamed with a polished sheen, its smooth curves hinting at the advanced technology hidden within. With a sense of anticipation, he poked his head inside, eager to explore its interior.

Within the confines of the pod, four seats, reminiscent of the heavy-duty bucket seats found in rally cars, awaited their occupants. But unlike their earthly counterparts, these seats were tilted slightly backwards, offering a sense of comfort and security amidst the chaos outside.

Heavy-duty straps and buckles adorned each seat, their purpose clear: to anchor the passengers in place in case of a tumultuous journey. The cockpit was centred around a small, flat disc resting on a plinth, its position just above the ground hinting at its importance within the pod's intricate machinery.

Despite his thorough inspection, Owen found no

visible means of control within the cockpit, leaving the tender's operation a mystery. But with no time to dwell on the unknown, he hurriedly ushered Jack and Sam through the door. They followed his lead and clambered into the seats, and Owen was about to follow them when—THUD! A bullet hit him in the forehead. He stayed upright for a second as a drop of blood trickled down his forehead, then dropped to the floor. Jack stared for a moment, then turned sharply to Sam.

"What just happened?"

He reached for the door, but Sam obstructed his path with her whole body. She put a hand out and tried to stay calm, expecting Jack to freak out at any second.

"Jack…"

"No! That did not happen! Owen. OWEN!"

As Jack tried to force his way past Sam, pistons hissed and the hatch closed firmly, trapping them inside. Failing to beat the closing door, Jack pushed his face to the window, trying to get a better look at Owen.

"He's gone, Jack. You can't help."

"NO! He'll be fine, we just need to get him in." He beat on the door, trying to see down the side of the tender for some sign of life.

"It's too late, Jack."

Jack pushed his forehead hard against the glass, as if trying to pass through, distraught at his inability to help.

"Why Owen? It should have been me."

"There's still time for that." Sam pointed out of the window at the walls. Jack wiped his eyes and looked up to see another section of the wall collapsing and pods falling over, some being swallowed by the hole.

Suddenly, Lawson appeared at the window, his body filling the entire frame as he thumped the glass with the side of his fist, causing Jack to lurch away. Lawson stared into the cockpit for a moment before spotting the oncoming collapse of the wall. As tenders fell like dominos, Lawson rushed for the next empty tender, quickly making his way inside.

Still wiping away the tears, Jack clambered back over Sam and into an empty seat.

"What do we do?" he asked.

"Give me your phone. I'm calling my mum."

As Jack struggled to get his phone, the disc in the center of the vehicle flickered, and a hologram of a man appeared. Sam immediately recognized him as the man Lawson had contacted at The Lodge.

"Welcome to the Phoenix 3000, and congratulations on having the foresight to prepare for such an unfortunate circumstance.

"In a few moments, we will be taking off. Please try to remain calm and allow the harnesses to strap you in. This is for your own safety as we will experience turbulence when leaving Earth's atmosphere."

The hologram flickered and changed to show a spacecraft. The straps and buckles automatically connected in front of their chests and tightened, as a rigid harness similar to those on a rollercoaster lowered over them, pushing them tightly into their seats.

"The journey will take only a few minutes before docking with our mothership, The Ark, which will transport us to our beautiful new home, the paradise planet, Kepler 186f."

The hologram flickered again, this time showing footage of luxurious homes automatically unfolding and assembling themselves.

"Everything you need for a luxurious life on arrival will be provided by The Ark. The journey will take many years, but be assured that The Ark's life support system will keep you in an extremely comfortable sleeping state as you travel.

"When you awake, you will be in paradise, ready to start life on a new Earth, unspoiled by pollution and overpopulation."

Jack and Sam looked at each other, speechless, as Jack passed his phone to Sam. The hologram returned to the man.

"In a few moments, a life support fluid will fill your cabin. Please do not be alarmed by this; it will ensure your survival. Try to breathe normally; the more relaxed you are, the easier it will be. Congratulations once again on your decision to join us in the new world."

As they looked at each other in disbelief, Jack started to panic:

"We need to get out! I definitely wasn't planning any space travel today!"

"I don't think we can. This thing is locked," said Sam, trying to push her harness off. "I need to get to my mum!"

"He said years! IN SPACE!"

Jack waited for a response from Sam, but she was distracted, looking straight past him. She pointed at the scene through the window. A black cloud was spreading quickly over London. As people were caught up in it, they started grabbing their throats and clawing at their skin as it began to blister.

"What is happening out there?" asked Jack as he followed her gaze.

"Pandora."

The walls of the tender reverberated with the thunderous roar of the engines as they surged to life, filling the cramped space with a deafening cacophony. Vibrations rippled through the pod, setting Jack and Sam on edge as they braced themselves for what was to come. Their apprehension turned to sheer panic as a strange, green liquid began to flood the interior, rising with alarming speed.

"GOO! Why's there goo?" Jack's voice was filled with fear, his struggles against the restraints growing more frantic with each passing moment as the level of the viscous substance continued to rise.

"Must be the life support!" Sam's voice cut through the chaos, her words tinged with a mixture of disbelief and resignation. "Shit, this is actually happening!"

"Holy shit!" Jack's exclamation was lost amidst the chaos as the pod shook violently, the walls reverberating with the force of the engines. Outside, other tenders met varying fates as they attempted to take off; some plummeting back to the ground, damaged and broken, while others thrashed about in a futile attempt to escape before crashing into the unforgiving wall.

As Jack and Sam's pod lifted off, the collapsing wall loomed ever closer, a grim reminder of the dangers that surrounded them. Amidst the chaos, Lawson's pod was caught in the maelstrom, dragged down into the ground below and consumed by a fiery explosion as its engines roared to life.

Inside the pod, Jack continued to struggle against

his restraints, his movements growing more desperate by the second. But Sam remained remarkably composed, her breaths shallow and controlled as she fought to maintain her calm amidst the rising tide of goo.

As the fluid crept ever closer to engulfing them completely, Sam held her phone aloft, her fingers trembling as she attempted to make a call. "Come on, come on," she muttered under her breath, her voice barely audible above the roar of the engines.

With each passing moment, the goo rose higher, threatening to engulf them completely. Sam's phone began to ring, the sound cutting through the suffocating silence of the pod as the fluid reached her shoulders. Desperately, she tilted her head back to prevent her mouth and nose from being submerged, her heart pounding in her chest as the call connected.

"Sam! Where are you! I've been worried sick! What's that noise?" Val's voice crackled through the phone, filled with concern and fear.

"Mum!" Sam's voice trembled with emotion as she struggled to find the words to convey their dire situation. But before she could speak, the goo surged upwards, rising above her head as she tried to speak.

With a final, silent gesture, she pointed the phone towards Jack.

"I don't. It's..." Jack's words trailed off as the

fluid filled the cabin, cutting off his words and stealing the air from his lungs.

As the goo closed in around them, Jack and Sam exchanged a final glance, their eyes filled with resignation and acceptance. Calmly, Jack released the air from his lungs and took a deep breath, allowing himself to be consumed by the suffocating embrace of the life support fluid.

PART TWO

Chapter One

A solitary tear traced a path down Sam's cheek as the circumstances of her arrival came into focus:

"So I'm here, what now?" Her voice wavered, betraying the fact that she wasn't sure if she truly wanted to hear the answer to her question.

"Now we must decide if you should remain," came the reply, a voice of authority tinged with an air of solemnity.

"Remain? How do I know if I want to remain? You haven't even told me where I am. The man said Kepler...?"

"We call it Eden," the response carried a sense of familiarity that caught Sam off guard, leaving her momentarily speechless.

"Eden? As in the Garden of...? Like in the Bible? You're not about to tell me I'm dead, are you? Because I definitely don't feel dead."

"Eden is the name of our planet," the voice clarified, cutting through Sam's confusion with matter-of-fact certainty.

"So we actually did go to space?" Sam's excitement and fear danced a delicate waltz within her, their steps uncertain and hesitant. "What happened to everyone else?"

"Many years have passed since you left Earth.

Your friends and family will be long dead," said the voice, warm yet somehow devoid of emotion.

Sam's breath caught in her throat, the weight of the revelation settling upon her like a heavy cloak.

"But Pandora—did it kill everybody?"

"A virus was released, and yes, most of the Earth's population died as a result. It appears that your own rulers believed the population needed reducing."

Sam's emotions churned within her, unable to settle on an appropriate state. The news of her mother's fate should have evoked a torrent of grief, yet she found herself strangely detached, grappling instead with the enormity of humanity's demise.

"It was done on purpose? No, that can't be right!" Sam's disbelief pushed aside grief for a moment to force its way to the front of the queue.

"It was not entirely deliberate: the perpetrators had not planned for it to be released before an antidote was ready, but yes, the virus was man-made for the purpose of selectively reducing the Earth's population," the voice explained, its tone measured and unwavering.

Sam fell silent as she tried to process this information, the weight of the revelation pressing down upon her like lead.

"You're talking about population control. Dad

used to talk about that. I thought he was mad."

"Your planet's resources were virtually depleted; it is not possible to maintain continuous economic and population growth on a finite planet," the voice reasoned, laying bare the grim calculus of survival. "Earth's leaders knew that and planned accordingly."

"So the people we saw getting into the escape pods, they were the selected ones? With their helicopters and limousines? Great, my family is dead, and I'm stuck here because of rich people."

Sam's bitterness laced her words as she thought of the injustices that had shaped her life up until this point.

"Anyway, how do you know all this? And why all the questions about how I got here if you already knew?"

"Perhaps you'd like to learn a little about us," the voice suggested.

As if from nowhere, a figure now stood in the room, graceful and ethereal, a portrait of beauty and exoticism. As she drew near, she extended a hand, beckoning Sam to join her at the edge of the disc.

"My name is Neem. Welcome to Eden."

With a flicker, the walls surrounding Sam dissolved, revealing a breathtaking vista. Sam found herself on a platform connected to a towering white structure by a slender walkway, her gaze drawn to a series of pristine domes set equidistant to form a circle around the tower, each with the same slender walkway. The best way she could describe the experience was like being inside a huge VR headset.

Moving cautiously to the edge of the platform, she found a futuristic city stretched out before her. It was a work of eco-friendly art: sleek, sustainable architecture seamlessly integrated into the lush landscape that surrounded it.

Towering skyscrapers, adorned with living walls of greenery, rose majestically into the sky, their reflective surfaces shimmering in the sunlight. Each building was a masterpiece of organically integrated design, harnessing renewable energy through solar panels, wind turbines, and geothermal systems allowing every inch of space to generate power, food, or oxygen.

Below, the streets pulsed with life but lacked the stress and crowding of London's streets. Automated vehicles glided silently along sleek thoroughfares, their passengers immersed in a world of tranquility and efficiency. Pedestrians strolled along tree-lined boulevards, amid stunning displays of flora that adorned the sidewalks.

Nature thrived in this harmonious metropolis, with verdant parks and botanical gardens interspersed throughout the urban landscape. Trees stretched skyward, their branches heavy with plump, brightly coloured fruit, forming a verdant canopy overhead, providing shade and food for pedestrians who casually helped themselves to snacks as they strolled.

Streams meandered lazily through the city, their crystal-clear waters teeming with life, while vibrant gardens burst with a riot of colour, attracting brightly coloured insects and birds in a mesmerizing dance.

As Sam strained to see the tiny people below, Neem suggested she try to touch them.

Feeling slightly ridiculous, she reached one finger out towards a small group sitting below a tree.

Sam gasped as she felt the gentlest of resistance, somehow like putting her finger in a pool of water but without getting wet. As she did so, she found her view altered; she was now within metres of the group she'd pointed at.

She recoiled her finger, and the scene reverted to her viewpoint from the tower. She repeated the motion to zoom in again and found herself transported, feeling the gentle breeze on her skin and smelling the flowers. This was no ordinary VR experience.

Having allowed Sam to take in the scenery, Neem now started to narrate:

"Over many years we have perfected our world,

freeing us from the tyranny of working for the profits of others. Our workforce is automated, requiring no payment. There is no money, no profit, no reason for greed. We want for nothing."

All around her, the residents engaged in artisan crafts, playing music, or creating artworks. As they pursued their interests, discreet robots performed the mundane tasks required to keep a civilised society afloat: cleaning the streets, collecting waste, delivering parcels, repairing signs, preparing and serving food, and harvesting fruit from the abundant orchards that surrounded the buildings.

"As technology takes care of our needs, we can focus on the higher disciplines," Neem continued, "Philosophy, art, music, care for our young and elderly."

It was not just the physical beauty of the city and its population that captivated her; from this viewpoint, she was overwhelmed by the palpable sense of peace and contentment that permeated the air. After so many years of tolerating the drudgery of London life, the struggle to simply stay warm and find food, she'd never imagined there could be a better way.

It appeared that in this utopian society, work was no longer a necessary burden but a source of fulfilment and purpose. Automation had liberated humanity from the drudgery of menial tasks, allowing individuals to pursue their passions and creative endeavours.

"The truth is that abundance is easily achieved with cooperation. Once we agreed to share resources effectively, working for a living became a thing of the past. We prefer to leave it to the robots."

As Sam gazed out over this idyllic cityscape, she was filled with a profound sense of hope. Here was a civilisation that had transcended the constraints of greed and selfishness, embracing instead the principles of cooperation, compassion, and stewardship of the planet.

It was a vision of what Earth could have been, a glimpse of its limitless potential had it just been treated with respect. It seemed so obvious now that she saw it, and it was that realisation that turned her hope into regret, as it dawned on her once again that Earth was no more.

Chapter Two

Jack stood at the edge of the platform, surveying the scene:

"So no one works? Sweet, I could get used to that... Hang on though, someone must have paid for all this to start off with – robots don't grow on trees."

"It is true that our planet wasn't always this way," said Neem, nodding solemnly.

The invisible walls of the dome flickered and briefly came back into view, morphing once again, this time placing them in a luxurious boardroom with impossibly tall ceilings.

"Many thousands of years ago, a very small and oppressive group called 'The Syndicate' controlled all of our planet's resources," she continued.

The room was adorned with towering pillars intricately carved with strange symbols and carvings, depicting tales of triumph and power. Stone walls adorned with golden motifs shimmered, polished to the point where they almost glowed, casting an aura of regal splendour.

Seated around an ornate table of polished ebony, men draped in ceremonial robes of deep sapphire and royal crimson gathered in hushed deliberation. Their expressions were grave, etched with the weight of responsibility and the burden of their decisions. Though their voices were muted, the tension in the air spoke volumes.

A large obsidian statue of a stern-faced deity loomed over the proceedings, its eyes seemingly penetrating the souls of those present, judging the actions unfolding beneath its gaze.

At the head of the table, a stern figure of authority presided, his bejewelled hand gesturing to signal the fate of the realm. Though the veneer of luxury and opulence surrounded them, the weight of their choices hung heavy in the air as their heads dropped and hands were reluctantly raised to vote.

"Our most valuable resource was Stone, mined from deep below the planet's surface. It provided building materials, fuel, and clothing. The Syndicate controlled the Stone and enslaved the planet by making life without it impossible. But Stone was a finite resource, and it became scarce."

As Neem spoke, the walls flickered and changed again to show the heart of a desolate quarry. The scene was one of harrowing misery and suffering; towering cliffs of rugged stone loomed overhead, casting deep shadows over the sprawling expanse below. Hundreds of weary workers toiled relentlessly under the scorching sun, their gaunt forms silhouetted against the harsh backdrop of the barren landscape.

The workers' hollowed cheeks and sunken eyes

displayed the unmistakable signs of malnourishment and neglect as they laboured under a burning sun, their tattered rags offering scant protection from the elements.

Jack became aware of the acrid scent of sweat and dust and covered his nose as it mingled with the pained groans of the workers. Overseers armed with clubs, chains, and assorted weapons, patrolled the quarry with ruthless efficiency. Whips cracked through the air with a sickening snap, meting out punishment to those deemed too slow or too weak to keep pace.

"Are they slaves?" he asked.

"That depends on your definition of slavery," replied Neem. "At the time they were considered employees, but they earned only enough to pay for basic food and accommodation, with nothing left over. Today we would define that as slavery."

"Sounds familiar," said Jack, thinking back to the life he and his friends had known.

Amidst the relentless toil, a worker faltered, their body succumbing to the merciless demands of their labour. They collapsed in the dust at Jack's feet, their feeble cries drowned out by the relentless rhythm of pickaxes against stone.

As an overseer lifted his club to beat the slave, Jack tried to grab his arm to stop the beating, but he fell straight through the hologram and the beating proceeded. Remembering this wasn't real,

Jack stood up and adjusted his clothing as Neem smiled and continued her story.

"Of course, this way of life was unsustainable. It was inevitable that the people would eventually rebel."

Another flicker put Jack in the middle of a large demonstration. In the urban sprawl, a wave of discontent erupted as impoverished and malnourished individuals took to the streets in protest against the unrelenting grip of capitalist exploitation. Their anger was clear, fuelled by years of economic injustice and systemic neglect.

At first, the protest was a gathering of weary souls, their faces etched with lines of hardship, their voices raised in defiance as they demanded an end to the relentless cycle of poverty. They bore banners and signs with slogans related to the struggles they endured in a society that valued profit over people.

But as the crowd swelled and their cries grew louder, the tension in the air became palpable. The arrival of a military force, clad in riot gear and heavily armed, only served to escalate the situation further.

Suddenly, chaos erupted. Smoke and gas filled the air, stinging eyes and choking throats, as the protesters found themselves engulfed in a maelstrom of violence and aggression. Shouts rang out, mingling with the sounds of shattering glass and stampeding feet, as the once-peaceful demonstration descended into turmoil.

In the midst of the melee, the most vulnerable bore the brunt of the brutality. Children cried out in fear, their small frames lost amidst the violence, while elderly protesters struggled to navigate the tumultuous terrain. Those who were malnourished and weak found themselves at a distinct disadvantage, their already fragile bodies ill-equipped to withstand the onslaught of force unleashed upon them.

Despite the overwhelming odds stacked against them, the protesters refused to back down. They stood their ground, defiant in the face of oppression, their resolve unyielding even as the forces of authority became more brutal.

"Despite the workers being greater in number, The Syndicate refused to give up their wealth and were too selfish to care about the impact of their actions. Rather than concede, they set about using the media to run hate campaigns, turning our citizens against one another."

The scene switched, revealing scenes of urban chaos and conflict as workers clashed with heavily armed authorities. Amidst the chaos, propaganda posters plastered on walls and billboards sowed seeds of division and mistrust among the populace.

"Divisions intensified, fuelled by propaganda that demonised dissent and glorified authority.

Neighbours accused each other of treachery, suspicion poisoning once-close communities. As the conflict escalated, violence and devastation unfolded. The global nature of the corporations meant that the conflict was soon worldwide."

Jack now found himself amid a huge rolling battle, with plasma shots taking huge chunks out of buildings and guerrilla soldiers being evaporated where they stood. It was all he could do not to run for shelter as the smell of burning flesh and molten metal seared his nostrils.

"It was amidst this chaos and carnage that a new threat emerged. As the rebellion spread worldwide, reports surfaced of foreign interference and manipulation. A power struggle between corporations and governments around the planet further exacerbated the divisions within society, each believing they had a better way to quell the uprising. Before long, the world was fully at war, with only one possible outcome."

With this, Jack's viewpoint rapidly zoomed out as though he was being dragged into space. He now watched as a series of huge explosions spread across the globe, the planet encompassed by a blinding light followed by a profound darkness. This was the inevitable conclusion of superpowers at war, a showcase of the destructive power of propaganda, division, and unchecked greed.

Neem gave Jack a moment to take in the horror of

the situation before continuing:

"Some survived for years underground, returning to the surface only once the toxic air had cleared. As society was rebuilt, we realised our only chance of progressing as a civilisation was to share our resources. What you see now is the result of our efforts."

The screens now showed people salvaging materials from wrecked cities; a valley entirely surrounded by mountains, where a small group of survivors were building self-sustaining houses sunken into the ground, growing plants and setting up solar panels. As though a fast-forward button had been pressed, time sped up and the settlement grew, spreading outwards as the population increased.

Chapter Three

As the room returned to its gentle white glow, Sam stumbled, disoriented by the rapid change in surroundings.

"What happened to The Syndicate? Were they punished for all of this?" she asked.

"The Syndicate could see no way to live without their wealth," Neem lamented. "They foresaw the climax of the war and came up with a plan that would allow them to continue their way of life elsewhere."

The room flickered again and Sam found herself in a vast aircraft hangar, with huge pyramid structures under construction. Neem continued:

"As the war raged on, they built huge, luxurious ships depleting the remaining Stone. They blamed different groups for the loss of the Stone, using the war to distract people from their hoarding. As the war reached its critical point, they poured all of the planet's remaining resources into their escape mission and abandoned Eden, setting off for a planet 15 million light-years away, just as life here appeared to be over."

Sam watched as huge slabs of land shifted sideways, taking trees and buildings with them, as massive hangar doors opened in the ground to reveal the vessels beneath. Slowly, almost majestically, colossal pyramids began to ascend from the depths below. Each one was an individual work of art, adorned with intricate hieroglyphs and glistening with an otherworldly sheen. Their sheer size dwarfed everything around them, casting long shadows that stretched far into the horizon.

With a low, rumbling hum, the pyramids ignited into motion, propelled skyward by a single massive rocket thruster at their base. The ground trembled beneath the power of their ascent as they soared towards the heavens, leaving behind a trail of ethereal brilliance that pierced through the night.

As they breached Eden's atmosphere, the pyramids converged with a colossal vessel floating in orbit, seamlessly docking with it as if drawn by some celestial magnetism.

Sam was now sucked inside one of the pyramids, to find a scene of eerie tranquillity. Rows upon rows of golden sarcophagi lined the walls, each containing a figure shrouded in frozen cryogenic sleep. Their faces were serene, frozen in a timeless slumber, while their bodies were encased in a soft golden glow.

"Unfortunately for them, the technology was not advanced enough. They were forced to put their lives in the hands of primitive cryogenic chambers, sleeping for hundreds of thousands of years. This had some consequences."

"So the people that caused the war just got away?" asked Sam, horrified by what she saw. "What happened to the people who were left behind?"

"In the aftermath of the war, the landscape bore scars of destruction, but amidst the rubble, a determined society emerged, fuelled by the collective resolve to rebuild. With a steadfast commitment to sustainability, we turned to the remnants of old technology, repurposing them into tools of renewal."

Once again, Sam found herself viewing a world in fast forward, as wind turbines rose like sentinels, their blades slicing through the air with a gentle hum, harnessing the power of the wind to generate clean energy. Across the horizon, solar panels glinted under the sun's rays, converting its abundant energy into electricity to illuminate homes and power machinery. Alongside, water wheels turned gracefully, drawing upon the force of flowing rivers and streams to supplement their energy needs.

"In the heart of this burgeoning society, a new ethos took root – one of cooperation and shared prosperity. Resources were distributed equitably, ensuring that no one went without the essentials of life. Communities worked together, pooling their skills and resources to construct sustainable infrastructure and cultivate fertile lands."

As time continued to speed by before Sam's eyes,

the scars of war began to fade, replaced by the verdant hues of rejuvenated landscapes and the steady hum of industry powered by clean, renewable energy.

"As our society advanced, we were able to truly cooperate for the first time in our existence. Building on existing technology, without profit as a goal, we progressed rapidly."

Sam found herself gliding through a gleaming factory floor, as a symphony of automation and innovation unfolded. Robotic arms, with precision unmatched by human hands, tirelessly assembled intricate components with meticulous accuracy. They danced in fluid synchrony, guided by complex algorithms and AI systems.

Meanwhile, in laboratories adjacent to the factory floor, scientists toiled excitedly, their minds probing the frontiers of possibility. They gathered around technological experiments featuring bright lights and speeding objects, pushing the boundaries of theoretical physics to unlock the secrets of warp drive technology.

A breakthrough triggered a moment of triumph that reverberated through the halls of the facility. With jubilant cheers, scientists celebrated as a successful result validated their theories.

The view returned to the factory floor, where the construction line had been replaced by a sleek spaceship, its hull gleaming with anticipation.

With a low, ominous hum, the vessel powered up its engines and gently rose up through the sky, safely above the gathered crowds. Some way above the clouds, the ship slowed to a halt and hovered, impossibly still, and then, in a dazzling display of light and energy, the spaceship vanished from view, disappearing into the vast expanse of space at warp speed.

"When we developed the Warp Drive, we realised we could catch up with The Syndicate and bring them back to Eden to stand trial for their sins. We arrived at their destination before they did and were able to observe as they attempted to start a new life."

Sam could now see satellite-like structures floating above a blue planet, awaiting the arrival of The Syndicate. As the vast mothership floated slowly into view and came to a halt above the planet, the satellites turned to watch as it jettisoned the pyramids towards the planet below.

The satellites moved again, some focusing on the mothership, others following the pyramids.

Chapter Four

Jack watched in awe as the pyramids fell towards the blue planet, their flat bases setting ablaze as they entered the atmosphere.

"So your ancestors did exactly the same as us then?" he asked. "Ruined their planet and left?"

As the pyramids fell towards the planet, Jack found himself falling alongside them, watching as the ornate decorations peeled off with the heat. As they broke through the atmosphere, huge parachutes opened to ease the pyramids' descent.

The fates of the pyramids were varied; some went into a spin as they broke through the atmosphere, burning and disintegrating before they reached the ground; some fell into the ocean; some were left to smash into the ground as their parachutes failed. Those that made it to the ground were scattered by the planet's rotation.

"We monitored their arrival; few survived," continued Neem. "Those that did were no longer themselves; centuries of sleep had damaged their minds and their bodies. They had no recollection of where they'd come from or how they'd arrived."

The scene was now at the planet's surface level, alongside a huge pyramid sat in a hot and dusty desert. A small hole had opened up in the side, from which people were crawling out, struggling to move, confused and terrified.

"We decided to observe their actions, to see whether or not they would recover and return to their old ways."

"Wait a minute," said Jack, "is that Earth? Are you telling me that your ancestors came to Earth?"

Jack walked amongst this disoriented group as they tried to make sense of their situation. They were clearly brain damaged and struggled to communicate with one another, fighting over food and shelter, hiding from each other amongst rocks and bushes.

"Not just our ancestors," replied Neem.

BONK! Jack hit his head, having forgotten where he really was and wandering into the desert but meeting the invisible wall of the room he was in.

As he rubbed his head, things finally fell into place for him. "Whose then, mine? Wait, you're human? But you're so..." he waved his arms around to suggest her size.

"Have you never wondered why the animals of Earth seemed so much better adapted than humans? Stronger, with no need to heat their food, comfortable surviving without clothes or man-made comforts? You may think of it as a sign of intelligence, but it's that intelligence which led to the destruction of your own habitat."

"Well, now that you mention it..."

"Your bodies were not designed for Earth; to survive, you needed to build and take far more of the planet's resources than indigenous mammals required. Eden is our home planet; the oxygen levels are higher, the gravity is slightly weaker, and our food is better suited. This makes us stronger, healthier, and much longer-lived. I would be 323 in Earth years."

"You don't look a day over 200!"

"Earth offered our species a chance of survival, but with it came a much shorter lifespan, weaker bodies, and disease. It seemed a fitting punishment to leave them where they were."

Again, time around them sped up. A basic society developed; dwellings were built, then temples, then cities. The scene switched between ancient cities around the world; Mexico, Egypt, China, Italy, Peru, Iraq, Nigeria, all showed similar scenes as civilizations developed.

In the middle of a desert encampment, a storyteller pointed to the heavens as a group sat around a fire, hanging on his words.

"Some had dreams of Eden, broken memories which they mistook for prophecies. When they told of their dreams, it resonated with their fellow travellers and formed the basis of many religions."

The group of listeners lay out flat in front of the storyteller, face down in worship.

"So God, religion, heaven, hell, all made up—I knew it!" exclaimed Jack. "I'm not sure whether to be happy or sad about that."

"Organised religion, yes. God? We have no way of knowing. We have no religion on Eden, no God to worship, but this is because we accept that it is beyond our understanding. Our values are built on community, compassion, cooperation, and love for our planet, rather than acting in search of reward or fear of punishment after death. We believe our actions should be judged during life. Selfish values have no place in such a society."

"Do you think I have selfish values?" asked Jack.

"You are descended from the worst of us, and brought up with a belief system entirely at odds with our own. It would be difficult for you to integrate..."

The screens returned to white.

Jack's enthusiasm for this new society was tempered slightly by her last sentence, leaving him with one last question.

"So what happens next?"

Chapter Five

Sam was concerned at the mention of integration; she'd heard it used by politicians in historical documentaries set before the rebellion.

"Are you an immigration officer?"

"Something like that. Many people would like to live here on Eden; it is a perfect society. We can't take everybody that applies."

"You could have mentioned that to me before I told my story. That was one day of my entire life, definitely the only day I ever killed anybody, and I really think I was pretty justified given the circumstances. You're not going to judge me on that, are you?"

"Your previous behaviour is a factor; we do not wish to allow criminals into our homes. The judgement we have made is that your actions were reasonable; you were not acting selfishly."

"Thank God for that, you had me worried."

"There are other considerations. We have a strict but fair immigration process on Eden, designed to help those who need it and protect those who are already here. Unfortunately, you did not follow the process, instead arriving in a small, untested ship without making the correct applications in advance of your journey."

Sam was nonplussed, her brow furrowed as she tried to make sense of what she was hearing.

"But... how... I don't... I didn't even know I was coming here! How could I have applied?"

"There is a process of application which, once approved, provides safe and legal routes to Eden. Unfortunately, your journey was organised for only the wealthiest people; they have all gone through the same screening process and, from what we have found, they are the worst that Earth had to offer. They've exploited others, stolen resources, and forced famines and wars. Even if they had applied correctly, they would never have been able to adapt to our society."

"But that wasn't me; I was one of the ones being exploited!"

"That may be the case, but these are the rules. You came here illegally; we cannot allow the unsafe trafficking of immigrants to yield success, or we would be inundated. There are many planets at war or at risk of famine in the Universe; we can only accommodate the most in need."

"So if we can't stay, what next? We have nowhere else to go!"

Chapter Six

The return journey had taken moments; they hadn't even needed seatbelts, so smooth had the transition from one galaxy to another been. The ship that carried them had a similar aesthetic to the interrogation room in which they'd spent so much of their visit to Eden. Softly glowing white walls with gentle curves made up the interior of the vast craft. Seats grew almost organically out of the floor, making instant adjustments to perfectly accommodate the many types of rears making the journey.

"We are about to enter Earth's atmosphere, please take your seats," came the instruction of a disembodied voice.

Jack was already seated with Sam, strongly aware of how little he had in common with his fellow passengers.

"I can't believe they made us leave!" he said. "You'd have thought such an advanced place would have a more enlightened view of immigration. They literally sent us back where we came from!"

"At least they didn't make us go to the nearest safe planet," Sam replied. "What did they say it was?"

"Can't remember. What do you reckon? Do you think Earth's safe now? You think the virus has gone?"

"I asked about that; you know what she said? Legally safe."

"What does that mean?"

"Who knows?"

"Well, I suppose we will. Very shortly."

As he spoke, the ship started to vibrate slightly and their seats moulded further around their bodies, holding them comfortably but securely. The vibrations turned into a shake as they entered Earth's atmosphere, and the chairs gripped tighter.

"I don't think I like this..." said Jack, resisting the urge to jump to his feet.

"At least there's no goo this time."

Jack had to agree it was preferable. As the shaking subsided, the sides of the chairs shrunk and released their grip.

"What about this lot, though?" Jack threw a thumb over his shoulder, towards their fellow passengers.

Most of them were elderly; despite the fact that everyone was now dressed in identical white jumpsuits, it was clear from their appearances that they were wealthy, and therefore landlords. Leathery skin, damaged by years of sun-drenched vacations, was pulled tight over their features, elongating their eyes and pulling the corners of their mouths too close to their cheekbones, their lips pumped up to counteract the thinning caused by the stretch.

"Who thought they were the best picks to repopulate the human race?"

"Money might have been a factor," opined Sam.

"You think?"

As they descended, the walls of the ship became transparent, revealing the planet below. At first, all that could be seen was the ocean, a huge swathe of blue that seemed never-ending.

"What happened to all the land?" asked Jack.

"We're probably over the Pacific," replied Sam. "It literally covers half the Earth's surface."

As the ship skirted across the endless blue, a coastline came into view. As they reached land, the ship steered to the left and travelled along the coastline.

As they zoomed by, they caught glimpses of familiar landmarks buried beneath the thick blanket of greenery that had reclaimed the land. Lost cities flashed by; skyscrapers, once shining reflective monoliths, long since relieved of the last of their glass, now nothing more than monstrous steel trellises entwined with ivy and vines.

Amidst the verdant landscape, glimpses of old technology peeked out from beneath the foliage, their metallic shells tarnished and rusted with age.

Crumbling remnants of highways and bridges stretched out like ancient ruins, their concrete foundations cracked and weathered by the passage of time.

But amidst the decay, there was beauty to be found. Nature had reclaimed the land with a vengeance, weaving its way through the remnants of human civilisation with a wild, untamed grace.

As they travelled, the landscape shifted and changed, revealing glimpses of the world they'd once known. A lighthouse stood sentinel on a rocky outcrop, its weathered facade battered by wind and waves. A dilapidated ferris wheel loomed in the distance, its rusted frame a stark contrast to the azure sky above.

"We must be in America," said Sam, pointing towards a huge statue that looked out to sea.

The Statue of Liberty stood as a lone figure amidst the ruins, her positioning saving her from the ever-creeping vegetation covering the rest of the land. Amidst the decay and destruction, there were signs of life.

"Look – people!" said Jack excitedly.

"I guess it must be safe then," replied Sam.

Small settlements dotted the landscape, their inhabitants eking out a meagre existence amidst the ruins of the old world. Smoke rose from chimneys, signalling the presence of human habitation amidst the desolation.

With a slight tilt, the ship turned inland, following a river towards a mountain range. Below, small groups of people could just be made out, pointing to the sky as they sped past.

After passing over a small forest, the ship slowed and hovered over a flat, open space at the base of a mountain. Slowly and silently, it dropped to the ground, emitting a loud hiss as the undercarriage doors opened and a series of feet appeared.

"Please make your way to the exit point," came the voice from the tannoy.

Joining the hundreds of elderly oligarchs making their way to the exit signs, Jack saw an opportunity.

"When we meet the people out there, we should tell them we're gods," he said.

"Drop it, Jack," was Sam's cool response.

"Space Police?"

Sam shook her head in despair.

"From the future then!"

"I can't believe I ever thought you might be useful. Of all the people I could have told about this, I had to pick you."

"Oh come on!" he persisted. "When do you ever get a chance like this?"

The wall ahead of them developed a horizontal split, which grew taller, as a ramp to the ground extruded itself from the floor. As they shuffled their way down the ramp, figures could be seen in the distance, cautiously appearing from the trees.

Along the length of the ship, more doors had opened up. Large containers labelled "MEDICAL", "ENERGY" and "AGRICULTURE", were rolling out of the ship and forming an orderly line. All at once, the containers opened up with a blast of steam, revealing large banks of robots, solar panels, farming equipment, and unrecognisable gadgets.

"At least they gave us a start," said Sam, as the robots came to life and immediately set about unpacking and organising, homes self-assembled and vertical farms built themselves up from the ground.

A group was now forming in the distance, pointing and clearly discussing their surprise guests, unsure whether to approach or hide.

"You think we should go and say hello?" asked Jack.

"What do you reckon? You think this lot are going to share this technology?" said Sam, looking back at their co-passengers. "Right now we're on their side; maybe we should take advantage of that...?"

Sam and Jack looked again at the collection of over-privileged, naturally selfish, landlord class that had paid their way into a new life, then back at one another. With nothing more than the certainty that they did not want to side with the landlords, they turned their backs on their fellow travellers and set off to meet the new residents of Earth.

The End

Printed in Great Britain
by Amazon